TENTH GRADE ANGST

Bruce Ingram

SECANT PUBLISHING

Salisbury, Maryland

TENTH GRADE ANGST

For information about this title, contact the publisher:
Secant Publishing, LLC
P.O. Box 79
Salisbury, MD 21803
www.secantpublishing.com

ISBN 978-1-944962-46-3 (paperback)

Library of Congress Control Number: 2018931870

Printed in the United States of America

This book is dedicated to my Lord Botetourt High School Creative Writing II-IV students who helped edit this book. Students with stars after their names formed a special group to work on the editing process.

Alexis Anthony*
Reese Austin
Haley Davis*
Maddy Deskins*
Jason Henderson
Noah Jarrett
Jessica Lancenese*
Mary Leweke
Abby Martin*
Luke Nackley
Kayla Olson
Samantha Queen
Anna Rosenberger*
Daphne Spangler
Courtney Stultz

This book is also dedicated to the following staff at Lord Botetourt who contributed help with editing, reading advice, and/or various chapters.

Carrie Baldacci, special education teacher
Doak Harbison, history teacher
Kendel Lively, librarian

Back
to
School

Chapter One: Luke

I have a girlfriend that likes me for who I am, and sometimes that's still hard for me to believe. Until Mia, my whole life I've always felt like a loser—and having Dad constantly tell me I wasn't ever going to amount to anything didn't help. A year ago I didn't even know whether I would stay in high school long enough to graduate and now because of Mia, I've definitely decided to go to college.

All summer, we worked together on our business. Mia came up with the idea and originally she called it L&M Lawn Mowing and Babysitting, Incorporated, where we would pool my mowing and her babysitting jobs together and if I could convince one of my mowing contacts to hire her as a babysitter, I would get 5 percent of the money, and the reverse would be true if she got me a new contact. Then we branched out to trimming shrubbery and selling eggs from her chickens, and over the summer we added selling fresh free range chicken and tree planting as part of our services. We will do just about any kind of job for money, as long as the place is close enough for us to ride our bikes to.

So Mia changed the name of our business to L&M Enterprises and she created a website and Facebook page. In the past year, I've saved a lot of money from our jobs and not using my money to buy school lunches to save every cent I can. Lots of times in the summer, I mowed three or four lawns in one day. I'm going to use that money for college or maybe one day have enough to buy some land out in the country.

I've always been in awe of how smart Mia is and I'm so excited about having our first real date this Saturday. It might be hard for somebody to understand that she's my girlfriend when we haven't had our first date yet, but her parents wouldn't let her go out until our sophomore year, so we've had to wait until Saturday. We decided back in the summer that we were going to ride our bikes somewhere, then go hiking and have a picnic. I'm in charge of the hiking destination (a place I know in the national forest) and she's in charge of the picnic food, and we haven't told each other what the other one has planned. She said that would be more romantic.

I haven't told my parents about Mia and am definitely not going to. Dad has a long list of "minorities who are ruining the country" and people from Mexico are on it—they're just about at the top behind blacks and Middle Eastern people. I thought about telling Mom, but she's just not right. All summer she's been sick and in bed, and she's been going to the doctor a lot. I've asked her a bunch of times what's wrong, but she won't tell me and keeps saying "nothing's the matter," but I don't believe her.

I'm really worried about Mom. If something happens to her, I'm afraid Dad will start drinking the hard stuff again and when he gets drunk... I don't want to talk about it. It would just be him and me, and that would be awful. Maybe I could go live with Granddaddy.

Mia has told me I have to have a better GPA than 2.0 (which is what I have) to get into most colleges, and she's right of course. She said for this year, her goal for me is to improve each class a letter grade. I don't know if that's possible. In ninth grade, I made a *B* in English and World History, and a *D* in Algebra I and Biology, and a *C* in everything else. Mia said if I had just done my homework in English and history, I could have gotten an *A* in both, and she's right.

But most days after school, I have to both take care of somebody's lawn and wash, wax or vacuum one of Dad's cars from his car lot business behind the house. By the time I get through with all that and eat dinner, it's after dark and I'm exhausted. I know I can get a better grade in ecology this year than in biology last year; and really I should have made better than a C in phys ed and health but the health part was just so freakin' boring. I mean, really, "the bones of the body" and "the function of the 'amazing' liver." But, Mia's right, I've got to make better grades and I'll try because she told me to.

I'll be 16 on December 10, so that means I can get my license on March 10. Mom took me a couple of times practice driving in our neighborhood when I got my learner's permit, but then she got sick, and riding in the car made her nauseous, so we couldn't go anymore. Dad took me driving once, and all he did was scream and cuss at me the whole time. My stomach was in knots anyway because I'm so inexperienced, and his yelling didn't help. I can't stand to be around him, and I think the feeling's mutual. He did say I could have one of his used cars to drive places, but it would be the "worst one," so in case I had a wreck, he "wouldn't be out much."

He also said that on weekends when he doesn't go to car races, we would start going to car auctions when I got my permit, and I could drive back the clunkers he bought. I don't want to do that. I'd rather go hunting or fishing or do something with Mia… maybe work somewhere for money. Dad never pays me anything; he says working for him is the price I pay for "living under his roof." This weekend auction thing is just going to be one more thing for us to fight about.

I don't want to live my adult life like my parents do. There's like this constant fear in our house that the money is about to run out. I've talked to Mia about this, and she said her mama said that "education is the way out." Well, I want "out." Mia makes me believe I can make it.

Chapter Two: Elly

I'm excited about school getting ready to start, but I'm not happy about how I look, my relationship with my boyfriend Paul, and this really hurts to say, but I need to... I fear that I've been shallow and lazy and maybe my parents have pampered me because I'm the only girl in our family. I want to do something about all these things this year.

I've started working on the appearance issue. Over the summer, I talked Mom into buying me contacts so I could rid of those awful mousy glasses that I've worn for years. It took me about a month to get used to the contacts, but now everything's working just fine in that department. But on the other hand, I gained four pounds over the summer and now I'm about 25 pounds overweight. I just don't see how I gained those four pounds. It must have happened when I was away at computer camp for two weeks. The food was really good and there weren't any scales around and I just maybe ate too much. Paul didn't even notice that I got contacts (which was depressing) and gained four pounds (which was good, I guess). On the other hand, he never really looks at me or talks about anything except his playing football, and "bulking up" because he's an offensive lineman—just stupid sports stuff.

I spent almost the whole summer at camps or on vacation with my parents. Enrichment camp, computer camp, gifted children of well-off parents' camp... those weren't their real names but that's what they amounted to. My family spent a week at the beach and later ten days touring places around the country. I was only home about three weekends all summer.

The only good thing about being gone was that I only had to go out with Paul twice all summer. He's not rough with me or anything like that and he's an okay guy, but the truth is, I don't feel anything when he kisses me, and I don't see this relationship ever going somewhere. Plus, kissing him is about as appealing as having sandpaper rubbed across my face. He either needs to grow a beard or shave his stubble, one or the other... gross! Over the summer, I began to worry that the only real reason I go out with him is because I fear that no one else will ask me out. That I just like the thought of having a boyfriend and having someone take me places. Which leads to me feeling—fearing— that I'm a shallow, insincere person, and I don't ever want to be that type person.

How do you break up with a guy? I've never done that before because Paul is the only guy I've ever gone out with. I've decided I'm going to talk to my best friends at school: Paige, Mary, and Mia, about how to do it. They've never broken up with anybody either but between the four of us, I hope we can figure out something.

I only saw Mia once all summer and that was when she and Luke came over because Dad hired them to "maintain and groom" our yard. They started work while I was still asleep and Dad told Luke to do other chores besides mowing until I woke up, which made Luke have to mow when it had gotten hotter. So I had eaten breakfast and was sitting in an air conditioning room painting my nails before I even realized they were here. I looked out and saw Mia trimming shrubs and Luke mowing, which made me feel lazy and worthless and guilty all at the same time. Like, they are sweating like crazy and I'm sitting inside in air conditioning with wet toenails. And that disgusting feeling of me being shallow just washed over me.

Finally, I decided to get dressed and come out and help Mia with the trimming, but as I was finding my shoes, I saw Luke stop mowing, bring some water to her, and motion for her to go sit in the shade and rest while he did her work for her for a while. Then she leaned her head into his shoulder, and he did the same, and then they hugged and held hands briefly, and I felt worse than ever about myself and my relationship with Paul. Why can't he show me tenderness like that? I want a guy like Luke, and sometimes I think I want Luke. Yeah, that would go over great with Dad, me dating the lawn maintenance boy from a poor family. And I would never try to steal a boy from a friend like Mia.

While Luke was doing Mia's work, I came out and talked to her about her summer. She was really glad to see me and said she had spent the whole summer working with Luke and doing her regular chores around the house and yard. When she asked me what I had done, I just said nothing much. I didn't want her to feel, well, *deprived*, if that is the word, because my parents have money to spend on things like camps and vacations. Then, I started feeling shallow again. I had to ask Mia if she and Luke had gone out on any dates, and she said no, that they were having their first date the first Saturday after the first week of our 10th grade year, which is when her parents said she could date. And I was again envious of her because she has someone she's really interested in, and I don't.

I decided that morning that I was going to try to volunteer somewhere for something. I ended up finding a volunteer job on Saturday mornings where, when school starts, I will tutor at risk kids for a local human services agency. I hope this will make me feel better about myself, and it will also help me get prepared for my job as a teacher when I graduate from college.

Chapter Three: Marcus

I should never have cheated on that history test last spring. My life has been screwed up ever since. It was bad enough that Coach Dell suspended me for the first two games of the football season because of the cheating, but then my girlfriend Tameka dumped me when she found out. Well, I think it was because of the cheating, it also might have had something to do with the fact that my parents grounded me for a month after they found out about my *D* in history for the year because of my cheating.

At the start of the summer, I blamed all my bad luck on getting caught and was ranting about that one day to my older brother Joshua when he said, "Your cheating had nothing to do with Camila and Kylee dumping you, maybe you'd better look a little deeper about what your real problem is—you're an insufferable little jerk."

At first I wanted to hit him, but then I remembered how he beat the crap out of me last May when all the cheating stuff happened, and I decided to back down. But, then, as time went by over the summer, I began to realize that Joshua was maybe right. I really hated to admit that to myself, but big brother was really right. I've got to grow up and take more responsibility for myself.

I also started to think about how many friends I really had and Caleb was really the only one. And even he is mad at me now because I'm his number one receiver on the football team and my being suspended is going to make things harder on him as the quarterback. So I apologized to him one day during summer workouts and told him I would try to make it up to him when I was back playing in games. He said he appreciated me saying that.

Then I decided to try to put things right with other people, starting with Mom and Dad. After dinner one night when Joshua had gone up to his room, I told them I was sincerely sorry for how I had been acting and would make it up to them by making better grades this year. I could tell Dad was skeptical, and he said I was still grounded for a month. He added that getting a car next spring (I've got my learners now) was still "under evaluation." I think he was surprised when I said all that, because I think he was expecting for me to argue with him, which, I admit, is what I've always done in the past. Mom said the best way for me to "show my good intentions" was to "honestly earn" an *A* or a *B* in every subject… preferably "more of the former than the latter." I said I would try, and I meant that, too.

I also sent an e-mail to Coach Dell and apologized to him and told him I would try to make it up to him and the team by my actions on the field. He responded immediately, and he said he would be looking forward to my putting my "words into deeds." I didn't apologize to Joshua. He criticizes me harsher than anybody, and wouldn't believe that I'm trying to change. But I'm going to show him, too.

I also texted Kylee, Camila, and Tameka, not all together but separately, and apologized for my behavior and said I was sorry for being immature when we were dating. Tameka didn't respond at all; she must still really be angry with me. All Camila texted back was "okay," which was at least something; she's probably still pretty ticked, too. But Kylee texted back that she was really glad that I was showing some "introspection" and that I had a lot of potential in life and sports if I were "more mature." That last comment really stung, but at least she thought enough about me to write. I waited a few days, so I could put my thoughts together, and texted back to her and said thanks and that she is a good friend. We've been texting at least once a day since then. I'm going to take it slow with her. I still like her a lot and maybe I could see if she would give me a second shot as a boyfriend. She's hot and smart, but she's also the type of girl that's not going to take any crap from any boy…which is probably the type of girl I need to keep me straight.

I've got Ms. Hawk for English 10 Honors first period again; she's the only teacher that I had last year that I will have this year. With about a month left in the summer, she sent out an e-mail to all her English 10 students about a summer reading assignment that she expected us to complete before school started. We had to read one of five books on the list and have a 300- to 500-word critical analysis on it done by the end of the first week of school. Usually I don't bother to read any of those summer reading books. It's always been so much easier to read online descriptions of them, take a few notes, then bluff my way through any kind of assignment.

But one of the books was named *Black Boy*, and since I'm trying to change my ways anyway, I read it… and it was really good. Maybe I've been missing out on this learning thing, too. The book is about a black kid growing up in the 1920s and rebelling against just about everyone and everything he comes up against. I've never read a book so good, but I've also never read most of the books I've been assigned. I'm going to try to get my act together.

Chapter Four: Mia

My biggest worry is that my poppa won't like me having a white boyfriend, but at least Mama is on my side now. All summer when Luke would come over to help me work on our business, I would make sure that he would come when Poppa was at work. For the longest time, I was worried that Mama didn't like Luke either, that she, just like Poppa, wanted me to date a Hispanic guy. But one Saturday morning while Poppa was at work, Luke came over to help me butcher two young roosters for us to sell to clients. We were going to drop off the meat on the way to one of our client's houses. I had been feeling bad all day, and I started to help him with the little roosters when I began throwing up.

Luke told me to go back inside and rest and he would take care of things. He came back late that afternoon and gave Mama a check for the two roosters and a check for my gardening work that he had done. Then, Mama told me later, Luke went into the henhouse and cleaned out the poop, which is what I have to do every Saturday. Mama said any boy who would do all that for me was worth hanging onto. She also finally confessed what I had already known... that Poppa couldn't stand Luke because he was white and lower class. So Mama said she and I would just keep the knowledge that Luke and I are going to start dating this year between the two of us...maybe that was the best way to handle things for now. Maybe over time if Luke were around Poppa a little, he would start to see the same qualities in him that Mama and I do.

Over the summer even though we only had to read one of them, Luke and I read all five books on Ms. Hawk's and Mrs. Kendel's summer reading list: *Black Boy, Salt to the Sea, Between Shades of Gray, Moby Dick,* and *Things Fall Apart.* Luke never would have read any of them before we formed our book club last year, probably looking up summaries of them on Wikipedia and using his writing skills to bluff his way through the assignment. But now, I can tell he really enjoys reading and we talked about which book we were reading at the time whenever we took a break from working during the summer.

Luke says he is definitely going to college now, which makes me really happy. Last year, I was scared he was going to drop out of high school when he got old enough. Like me, he has really been saving his money for the future. He talks all the time about buying land out in the country and living there one day, and I think what it would be like to live out there with him. It would be so romantic.

I know I'm too young to fall in love and to know what love is. I want to find a man who is kind and sweet and makes me feel safe and secure and wants to have children and be a good husband and father. Luke might be that man one day, I don't know. He has all the things I'm looking for, and I'm just going to enjoy being with him and see what the future brings.

When we have our first real date this coming Saturday, we're going somewhere in the national forest on a picnic. I'm in charge of the food, and Mama and I decided that *arroz con pollo* would be a good choice. I'm going to devil some eggs, too. Luke said he would take care of dessert by gathering some wild berries; for me just to bring the main course and whatever else I wanted to bring. He knows everything about the outdoors. I bet we're going hiking up in the mountains somewhere. Mama says she trusts him to be alone with me. She knows he has a good heart after being around him this summer.

Mama and I talked a lot this summer about my future education. I know how much she likes being a nurse, but I think I want to become a doctor and that's what she has encouraged me to do. I think I would like to be a pediatrician and work with little kids but I know that I would need four years of medical school after college, and then I would need to be in residency at least three years. I also know my family doesn't have the money for all that. Mama said that she and Poppa are expecting me to be the valedictorian of my class and that that would lead to scholarships. I know that, but I'm not going to be obsessed with being the best student in my class. That would make me all stressed out. I'm going to try to do the best I can, and I think things will work out. I know I can make an *A* plus in everything.

I start and end the school day with Ms. Hawk and English 10 Honors first period and Yearbook seventh period. I am going to be in charge of features for Yearbook, which should be fun. I have World History II second period then Ecology, Geometry, lunch, Phys Ed 10, and French II before Yearbook. I have Luke in my first, second, third, and seventh period classes, and we're going to sit together. He asked me to tutor him on Tuesdays and Thursdays during lunch, just like last year, and then on Fridays, we can have our book club meetings. Luke got put in the "general" Geometry class fourth period; he said it's for the "stupid in math" students, which was a little harsh but pretty accurate. I'm hoping I can get him through that class, but I'm not very sure I can.

First Day
of
School

Chapter Five: Luke

I got to first period English 10 Honors class early because, well, I was actually looking forward to it…which is hard to believe that I like some things about school. Ms. Hawk smiled at me when I came in and said she had "big plans" for me in Yearbook as sports editor. Soon afterwards, Mia came in and sat down beside me and showed me a computerized printout of our jobs for the next month and how we would work them around school and homework.

I noticed that this Saturday between 10:00 and 4:00 P.M. was left blank and all the other Saturdays of the month were the same way for those times, and I asked her why those blocks were open, and she looked at me and smiled and said that I knew what those open periods were for and stop pretending that I didn't. That's when we can have our dates and still have time to do jobs in the morning and evening.

English class went great, and so did World History II and Ecology, but the day just fell apart after that. Geometry was filled with kids just like me, people stupid in math that didn't want to be in there. About five people, all guys, came in late, and it wasn't because it was the first day of school—nobody was in a hurry to arrive in purgatory. Then the teacher, she said her name was Ms. Waters and that this was her first teaching job, introduced herself and talked about the "importance of geometry in our daily lives." Oh, yeah, right, geometry is the one thing that's been missing in my life, and if I only had geometry, life would be great when Dad is cursing at me. Why does the school give all the new teachers the hardest to teach students in the hardest to understand courses?

Then that woman started talking about the "Parallel Postulate," how "that through a point that's not on a given line there is exactly one parallel line." Aughhhhhhh. What's that supposed to mean? How in any known universe on any known planet can a point somewhere off in space somewhere have a line that is parallel to it and then have that line find that point and then run right through that point, and how is it still parallel to it if it is running through it?

I am still trying to wrap my mind around all this junk when Ms. Waters came up with another pearl of wisdom, that "concepts of congruence, similarity, and symmetry can be understood…" (No, I don't understand them) from perspectives of the "fundamental rigid motions" and "translation." I understand the word translation and that geometry is a foreign language designed by evil aliens on a hostile planet that have come here to suck the life blood out of us. I'm not sure I got all that right, she was going so fast and I'm so stupid, and half the class was checking their phones or texting while all that was going on, and the other half was sitting in stunned disbelief that they were going to need to understand this crap to pass the class. I got no chance to pass this class.

I had lunch next, and Mia had offered to come to the library and sit with me at a computer and for us to be together, but I told her that I didn't want to monopolize all her lunch periods, and she needed to sit with her friends on Mondays and Wednesdays. I meant that, too. I don't want to be one of those possessive boyfriends. We can have Friday lunches to enjoy being together because there's not going to be much joy when she's tutoring me in geometry on Tuesdays and Thursdays.

Things continued their downward spiral when I got to Phys Ed and Health fifth period. After my mind was about to explode from the geometry, I needed to go outside and run or play some kind of game with a ball, anything to clear my mind. Instead, I found out that we were going to do health this week, and Coach Miley said that today's topic was "sports rules." What about how to drive a car, when is that supposed to happen? I need that information with Mom too sick to help me with my driving and Dad too angry and busy to take me. A fifty-five minute lecture on "what you should know about volleyball rules" was what we got instead. The lecture was highlighted by the world's longest and most boring PowerPoint in recorded history. (I mean, does each bullet point have to be four lines long and can't there be at least one picture on a slide. Everybody is just dying to see a picture of a volleyball on the screen.) Spanish I was next, and I didn't understand much what Ms. Hurst was saying because she's from Germany and still speaks with an accent from that country, and she was introducing us to the most common Spanish sayings, which would be confusing enough without her accent. I'm not worried about Spanish, though, Mia will help me with that.

Yearbook was great. Mia, Elly, and I are on the same team. Elly is going to take most of the pictures for Mia's features and my sports coverage, so I get to work with the two nicest, prettiest girls in the whole school. Being with them and making plans for what we were going to cover almost made me forget what I had to do after school. As soon as I got home, I had to go mow a lawn two streets over, and I felt like I was running across the grass just to get it done in time, so I could trim the shrubbery and get home so I could wash one of Dad's cars before dark and then get it vacuumed.

I finally finished all that around 8:30 and then I remembered that I hadn't eaten since I had an energy bar for lunch, and I looked for Mom and she was already in bed asleep, which is where she is much of the time it seems. I'm really worried about her, something terrible has got to be going on. I looked in the freezer and all there was were macaroni and cheese packages (which I can't stand because we have it for dinner all the time) and packages of cheap pizzas, which have something in them that give me hives. The refrigerator part was highlighted by rows and rows of Dad's favorite beer, some Jack Daniels when he is feeling particularly festive, and some milk that had one day left on its expiration date. I had had a feeling that Dad had become reacquainted with Mr. Jack because of the way he's been acting lately.

I found two very brown bananas, some stale cornflakes, and with the milk about to go bad, I ate and drank every bit of that stuff. I'll try to get up early tomorrow morning and run my usual three miles and work on my English and World History homework. I'm not going to even bother with the geometry homework. I'll tell the teacher I didn't understand what I was supposed to do, which will be the truth. Knowing the students in that class, I'm sure tomorrow there's going to be a long line of zeroes for homework scores in the gradebook. She can't fail us all, can she? If I keep my mouth shut and don't act up, I bet she'll pass me on with a *D* just to get rid of me.

I'm guessing the refrigerator fairy is not going to visit overnight and stock up the old icebox. So what's going to be on the breakfast menu? I guess that it will have to be that stash of energy bars that I keep under my bed. Yep, this is how I sure want to live when I'm an adult. Ain't life grand!

Chapter Six: Elly

I got to first period English a little early so I could make sure that I did my summer reading assignment on *Salt to the Sea* correctly. I was glad to see Ms. Hawk, and I'm proud that she had enough confidence in me to make me the photography editor. I showed her the new Nikon that Dad bought me and she said for me to use that camera since it was way better than any she had for the class.

I was still chatting with Ms. Hawk when I saw Caleb come in and sit by himself, so I thought here was my chance to show him how much better I look without glasses. I totally forgot that I'm dating Paul; I'd dump Paul in a heartbeat if Caleb would notice me just a little, and if I thought I had any chance with him—he's so good looking and athletic and the quarterback (I don't know much about sports but I know that's a big deal) and …that long wavy hair of his! So I ended my conversation with Ms. Hawk and went over and sat down next to Caleb and fidgeted around for a minute or so, waiting for him to say hi or something, but he was so busy texting that I don't think he had even noticed that I sat down.

I waited another minute or so, and he still hadn't noticed me, so I said something lame like, "Did you have a good summer?" And his response was "Yeah," and kept on texting. He didn't even add "did you" to his "yeah," and he still hadn't looked up to notice how different I look now. I waited another minute or so, and there weren't any more comments from him, and I was desperately thinking of something to say and I came up with, "How's football going, are you ready for the first game this Friday night?" This time, he mumbled something; I couldn't even hear what he said. And then I looked over and saw that Paige and Mary had come in, and Paige made eye contact with me, frowned and shook her head and motioned with a hand for me to come over and sit with them. Mary had this smirk on her face, like she was saying that I was making a fool of myself.

I was about ready to get up when Caleb practically leapt out of his seat because this girl came into the room. She must be a new student, because I had never seen her before, and she was absolutely stunning: long jet black hair and long legs and she was wearing a really short skirt. How did Caleb see her out of the corner of his eye from across the room and not even notice me while I was sitting right next to him? Who am I fooling, I think we all know the answer to that question. I got up and slouched over to Paige and Mary, and Paige whispered out, "Stop torturing yourself about him," and Mary in typical blunt Mary fashion said, "Give it up, you look desperate."

I felt absolutely humiliated by what they said, especially Mary's comment, but they're right...I've got to put Caleb out of my mind. I was so mad at myself and kept replaying the whole thing over and over in my head. Time went by and Ms. Hawk was welcoming us to class and showing the class syllabus on the Smart Board, and I was still obsessing on Caleb and my misery. Then Ms. Hawk called on me to read from the literature book, and I asked her where we were in the story, that I had lost my place and then a bunch of people, mostly the boys, started laughing. Ms. Hawk said we were at the beginning of the story, and then the guys laughed again.

So in the first minutes of the school year, Caleb ignored me and the rest of the boys in first period laughed at me. I know my face was red and it got even redder when I realized I was so out of it, I hadn't even heard Ms. Hawk say the page we were on, and I had to ask her and this time her voice was a little sharp when she said "Page 32." I stuttered and stammered my way through two paragraphs before Ms. Hawk cut me off (we usually have to read four or five paragraphs in her class) and asked somebody else to read. Great, now I've also made my favorite teacher mad at me... can this day get any worse?

The next three periods were just a blur, I was so upset and mad at myself, and I couldn't seem to focus and kept replaying in my head over and over the start of first period. When lunch came, I went over and sat with Paige, Mary, and Mia. Paige and Mary were talking about what they were going to do Friday night, Paige saying that Allen was going to take her out for pizza before they went to the football game, and Mary said that she and I were meeting Richard and Paul after the game for food wherever the guys wanted to go.

Mary then smirked and said that's what she thought we were doing, unless "Elly wants to wait outside the guys' locker room and wait for Caleb to notice her." Then Paige said "Stop it, Mary, that's enough, it's getting old," which made me think that I had been the topic of conversation before I got there.

Mary's one of my best friends, but she's got this cruel streak in her that comes out every now and then. I decided to take the high road and say I deserved to be made fun of after "my performance" in first block and then Paige said, "Who's the new girl that Caleb was so interested in?"

Of course, like always, Mary knows everything about everybody and said the girl's name is Amber. She's a transfer student from India, and her dad just got a job as a doctor at the hospital and her mom will be a professor at the community college. Great, another smart, pretty girl in honors' classes where there aren't enough guys to go around anyway.

Chapter Seven: Marcus

It's been hard practicing with the guys the last couple of weeks and knowing that I can't play in the game Friday night. Coach Dell put me on the scout team during scrimmages so I could run routes that the Springfield receivers do. It's no fun running simulated plays of the team we're facing, meanwhile watching Caleb and Joshua and the rest of the guys prepare for the game. It was almost a relief for school to start, so I could think about that and get my mind off not being able to play the next two Friday nights.

The first day back, Dad surprised me and asked if I wanted to drive to school so I could get some of my driving hours in, then he could take over and go on to his office. Dad bought a new BMW over the summer, and, yeah, I want to drive that car around. He's started to ease up on me a little bit because I think he can tell that I'm sorry about the cheating thing from last spring and am trying to do better this year.

While we were driving through our neighborhood, all of a sudden Dad said, "Slow down, let's practice your parallel parking." He pointed to two cars parked out on the street and there were like three spaces between them, so there was plenty of room for me to do all that backing and twisting of the steering wheel to get the car in next to the curb. I thought the whole parking thing was going to be easy. I'd just pull up to the front car and start backing up, then cut the wheel so that the car would slide into the space. But as I was starting to back up, Dad suddenly yelled out that I was about to hit the car, and I said, "You're crazy," and he yelled out, "Stop the car, right now, and get out."

He was so mad I decided not to say anything else, and when we got out, I saw that the left side of our back bumper was only a few inches away from a neighbor's car and our new BMW was about to hit it. If I had kept on going, I would have hit it for sure. I apologized to Dad, and he calmed down. He said we could go practice parallel parking on Sunday morning when the streets were quiet. This driving thing's going to be a little harder than I thought.

I got to Ms. Hawk's first period English 10 Honors class early and turned in my paper on *Black Boy* four days before it was due. I could tell Ms. Hawk was impressed that I was already done with the paper, and she thanked me for getting it in early, so she wouldn't "have so many to grade at once." Then she told me something that both made me feel good and bad about myself. "Marcus," she said, "you know, you have a lot more ability than you showed me last year. Give me more effort this year and read the material, and I'll bet you find that you even like to read."

If everything we read was as good as *Black Boy*, she's probably right, and I told her so. The paper I did for her on that book was the first one I've ever written without getting tips on what to write about from online. I then went to look for a seat in the circle of desks that she'd already arranged and decided to sit next to Ms. Hawk, so I would pay more attention to what was going on and not be distracted by Caleb. To my surprise, a little while later Kylee came in and sat down beside me and smiled and started chatting. We found out that we had both read *Black Boy*, and she had liked it as much as I did. I'm going to take it slow with her or any girl I'm interested in this year. It's going to be a while before we can get to the "talking" stage, I would guess, let alone start dating. I hope she will give me another chance.

After the introduction to the class thing that most all teachers give, we started reading a short story, "The Bass, the River, and Sheila Mant." Ms. Hawk had me read second, and I was embarrassed because I had trouble pronouncing some of the words (*epitome* and *suave*) or didn't know their meaning (*incarnation*). I was even more embarrassed when Luke and Mia, one or the other, either gave the correct pronunciations or the definitions to all those words—words that they seemed to know just like that. My first thought was that, "Oh great, a poor white boy and a poor Mexican girl are showing me up now." But then, I started to think that maybe I had been a jerk to lower class kids in the past and maybe that's something else that I needed to change about myself. Those two are always hanging out together; is there something going on between them? I've really never paid any attention to either of them. I'll say one thing about Mia, she's hot.

Next, I went to World History II, and I started to immediately worry that the teacher, Mr. Wayne, had been told about my cheating last year and would have it in for me before school even started. But if he did know, he didn't let on when he went around the room to make a seating chart and briefly talk to each of us and get to know us a little bit.

The rest of the day was pretty much the same in every class on the first day: long lists of rules, mostly with the word *don't* in them, followed by seating charts, a syllabus, and a lecture, in other words... borrrrrring.

Chapter Eight: Mia

Mama said I could wear a little makeup this year, so I put on some mascara, and I was so hoping that Luke would notice when I sat down next to him in Ms. Hawk's class. He said I looked great this morning, and I know I must have beamed, and I sat down and squeezed his hand. I think he did notice! We were talking about our picnic date on Saturday, and he was still being mysterious about where we were going to go; when I kept hearing this rumbling sound, and then I finally realized it was coming from his stomach.

I asked him if he had eaten breakfast and found out that all he had eaten was an energy bar because there was hardly any food in the house, but "plenty of booze" was what he said. I know he's told me that his mom is sick, but I have a feeling it's worse than what he's let on...or maybe he doesn't know how sick she is. Right then, I decided to make him an egg and cheese sandwich tomorrow morning and bring it to him first period. He can't do well in school if all he eats for breakfast and lunch are two energy bars total. And we have jobs to do every day after school this week, which just makes things worse for him. If I told him I was going to bring him some food, he would tell me not to, so I'm not going to tell him.

I've got a busy week with studying and work. I've got to deliver eggs Monday and Thursday after school, yard and garden maintenance work on Tuesday and Wednesday at houses where Luke is mowing, and babysitting Friday and Saturday nights. Saturday morning, I have to clean out the henhouse and then help Mama clean our house. She knows I need to be done by 8:30, so I can prepare the *arroz con pollo* and get myself ready for our—my first ever—first date.

I'm not at all nervous about going out with Luke. At lunch Monday, Elly and Mary said they were really nervous about their first date, but Paige said she really wasn't because she and Allen were friends before they went out for the first time, and they've been a couple ever since. I think that's how things should be, that you should be friends with a guy before you go out with him. That way, you won't make the mistake of going out with someone who's absolutely no good for you.

I want my first date with Luke to be special, and I know it will be. I know we will have lots to talk about because we always do. There's one thing that I really want and that is for him to kiss me. All summer when we were working together, we were always so dirty and sweaty all the time that it just wouldn't have felt right if we had kissed then. But now it would feel right.

What happens, though, if we've been together all day, and it's almost time for our date to be over and Luke hasn't kissed me? Should I show him in some kind of way that I want to be kissed? But Mama always says not to be too forward with boys, so I can't act like that toward Luke. I think maybe the best thing is just to act around him like I always do, and let things play out naturally.

I've been thinking about how to wear my hair Saturday. Luke often compliments me on my long, dark hair, and I always wore it in a ponytail when we were working, so I want to wear it loose and natural Saturday. But we have to ride our bikes somewhere, and it's probably going to be hot...maybe I should put my hair in a ponytail while we are riding to wherever we are going, then let it loose?

Another big topic at lunch Monday was Amber, the new girl. Mary was teasing Elly pretty hard about making a fool of herself with Caleb, and him getting up to leave when Amber came in while Elly was still trying to talk to him, and from the look on Elly's face, she was upset about the whole thing. Paige asked me what I thought about all that, and I said I hadn't been paying attention because Luke and I were going over our jobs for the week. High school kids make too big a deal about all this social interaction stuff; most students most of the time aren't paying attention to this stuff that one of us thinks is so important.

Then Mary said I should be worried about Amber, too, and I said, "I don't see why." And she replied that Amber was really smart and could be my competition for valedictorian. I'm not going to spend my time worrying about something like that, either, and I told Mary that. If I study and do the best I can, and I will, things will turn out okay, and I told her that, too. The most important thing is to earn scholarships for college because I know my parents haven't been able to save a lot of money just for me, especially with my two younger sisters going to need help for their education, too, one day.

It was about then that I realized I had spent too much of the day thinking about things other than school, so I decided to put the date, and jobs, and Elly's problems out of my head and concentrate on my classes.

In fifth period, I took lots of notes about the body's organs and tissues because I'm going to need to know all that information for when I'm in medical school. In French II sixth period, we got 20 new vocabulary words, but I already basically knew what about 15 of them meant from similar words in English and Spanish. Last in Yearbook, Luke, Elly, and I made our plans for the spreads we have to finish this nine weeks in order to meet our deadline. Then it was time for me to go home and deliver eggs.

The
Weekend

Chapter Nine: Luke

Saturday, I was so hungry when I got up, and there still wasn't much in the refrigerator. I looked in the freezer and way back at the back were some frozen walnuts under the macaroni and cheese package and an almost empty package of peas behind the ice cube tray, so for my entrée I dined on peas with walnuts—sure to become an instant breakfast classic. I can't stand macaroni and cheese; we've had it for years for too many dinners and I'm not going to have that crap for breakfast, too.

I had to mow two lawns, ours and a neighbor's, before leaving our house at 9:30 and riding my bike to meet Mia for our date. I mowed ours first, so that Dad wouldn't yell at me for not having it done when he got up, and so he would also see that I was busy and not tell me to do some kind of car chore. I was hoping that that he would leave for some car lot to look for bargains while I was mowing, and, luckily, that was what happened, which was a big break for me. I sure as heck couldn't have told him that I had a date with a Hispanic girl as the reason I couldn't help with something.

When I got back from mowing the neighbor's lawn, nobody was around, and I checked the refrigerator again with the hope that Mom had gone and come back from the grocery store, but the fridge looked as barren as usual. I saw that the door to Mom and Dad's bedroom was still shut, so I thought maybe Mom was still in there, so I knocked to see if she was all right. She didn't answer, so I opened the door to peek inside, and she was still asleep. And then I walked in to say I was leaving to go somewhere, and I looked at Mom and she was bald and there was this brown wig on her bed stand. Then it hit me, Mom's got cancer… no, no, no, oh no. That explains why she's in bed all the time, she must be getting chemotherapy. And that explains why Dad is angrier than usual and has started back drinking so much. What if Mom dies? What would life with just Dad and me be like? I'm scared of him now, he would be an absolute terror if Mom were gone. He might take his loneliness out on me. Then I felt guilty about thinking of myself first when I had just found out that my mother has cancer. What should I do, what should I say to her… that I love her and want her to get better? But she didn't want me to know. Was she worried that I would worry about her? I didn't know what to do or say to her. Should I ask Mia for advice, should I tell her about Mom?

I tell Mia everything, and she's always so willing to talk about things… to help me out. I wish I could help her like she helps me. I backed out of Mom's room, and went to the kitchen to get a baggy and put sugar in it for the wild blackberries that Mia and I were going to pick for dessert and got on my bike and left.

When I met Mia, she had this big smile on her face, but then she looked at me as if she were reading my expression, and said, "What's the matter, what's wrong, tell me." I got worried that she thought I didn't want to be with her, and, really, Mia is the best thing in my life. So I told her everything was fine, which wasn't the truth… that I had been rushed all morning, which was the truth. I decided to hide Mom's cancer from Mia, so she wouldn't worry about me, and how I was coping. I gave a forced smile and said to follow me and about 30 minutes later we were at one of the access roads to the national forest.

After we had hidden our bikes in some undergrowth, she walked over to me and said, "Luke, we're not taking another step until you tell me what's bothering you."

I said nothing and I started to cry. It was humiliating. Here I was on my first date ever and I'm crying in front of a girl that I really care about. I had been thinking about and looking forward to this day for months, and I was so worried about losing Mom; then Dad and I would be alone in that house and how awful that would be—I just had a rush of emotions that burst out. I finally got my crying under control, and I told Mia the whole story, and the entire time we were sitting on a rock and had our arms around each other. When I finished, she said, "I'll help you get through this," and, I said, "I really appreciate that," and I know that she will be there for me.

Then suddenly she said, "I've got an idea. Why don't you talk to your mom and tell her that you know that she hasn't been feeling well lately. You don't have to tell her you know about the cancer. And tell her that to take some of the pressure off her and Dad and taking care of you, what would she think about your going to live with your granddaddy on weekends until she is feeling better."

Mia said that on weekends, I would get three meals a day with Granddaddy, be away from Dad, and I could arrange with the school secretary to ride to Granddaddy's house on a different bus on Friday evenings and Monday mornings. It would be a win-win for everybody.

Mia also went on to say that she knew I wasn't getting enough to eat, that was why she had brought—and was going to continue to bring no matter what I said—something to eat before school every day. And again, she emphasized, I was not to tell her not to do that. I've felt guilty about her bringing me those egg dishes this week, but it's also felt good to have something to eat. Mia is so smart, and I told her I really liked everything she had said and was going to talk to Mom about it.

And then there was this pause, and I looked at her and she looked at me, and I kissed her for the first time, and she gave me the biggest smile.

Chapter Ten: Elly

Mary's and my double date with Paul and Richard was a total disaster. Having to go watch a sport that I know nothing about and care nothing about was bad enough, but we had to get there at 6:30 to get ready for the 7:00 start and then after the game was over around 9:30, we had to wait until after 10:00 for the guys to meet us. So it was almost four hours of waiting around, so I could watch Paul and Richard stuff pizza in their faces for thirty minutes. I didn't really want anything to eat but Paul insisted that I have a couple slices from his pizza, which meant that I had two dinners that night, and that's exactly what a girl who is 24 pounds overweight needs to be doing.

Meanwhile, Paul had to explain that "we" had lost the game because the referee had flagged him twice for holding, which was "so unfair" and the "the refs sucked." Who was Paul holding or what was he holding. I thought the quarterback held the ball most of the time, was Paul holding Caleb? If so, why would he be doing that? Football is so stupid. That was followed by a drive to a cul-de-sac near my house so that Paul and I could make out in the front seat and Richard and Mary "went walking." There's nothing like kissing someone with fresh pepperoni breath and four-day-old stubble to make a girl feel good about herself... meh.

The evening was made perfect when Paul announced that we—the four of us—were going to play video games at his house Saturday night and watch some college football games on TV—that he and Richard were going to pick Mary and me up at 6:00 after they had picked up some pizzas. Isn't he going to even ask me if that's what I would like to go do? Apparently, I have no say about where we are going to go or what we are going to do. So Saturday night will be Round II of pepperoni flavored kisses, but this time with five-day stubble. And don't forget that all this romance will be paired with watching, now wait for it...college football! Yippee!

When I got home, I texted Mary to see if she wanted to talk, and she called me almost immediately. I told her that I was thinking about breaking up with Paul, that there was no future in this relationship, and I dreaded, yes dreaded, the thought of spending hours and hours at his house watching him and Richard eat and watch TV and yelling at the screen. Mary told me that I shouldn't break up with Paul because, then, I might not have a date for homecoming. Which I thought was a really stupid reason for continuing to date someone.

Mary has been one of my best friends for a long time, since grade school, but her comment was just ridiculous. And maybe I should stop relying on her so much for advice. There's nothing wrong with accepting a date with some guy just because you're bored and want to get out of the house. I mean, I could understand, me, or one of my friends, saying yes to a guy just to get out and do something and see what the guy was like. But to continue to go out with someone when there's no future in the relationship... I think that's wrong.

After Mary's comments, I won't call it advice because it wasn't worth anything, I texted Paige and asked if I could call her and she texted back, yes, that she was still awake. I called and told Paige about my evening and the plans for Saturday night, and my whole boring relationship with Paul, and she was very sympathetic about my situation. She said that maybe I should break up with Paul, or maybe I should give him a chance to change and ask him to not be so bossy and let me make some decisions about what we should do on dates, or at least run some dating plans by me before making a decision. Her advice was sincere, but I'm not sure I want to spend time "fixing" Paul; we just have nothing in common. I started to call Mia, but I figured she was in bed already (she still doesn't have a cell phone so I can't text her), so I decided to call her Saturday morning.

I called Mia about 9, and she said she didn't have much time to talk because she was getting ready to meet Luke for their first date. And I could hear the excitement in her voice and once again, I felt a twinge of jealousy toward her, which made me feel awful about myself for being jealous of her and Luke—and also awful about being stuck in a mind-numbing relationship. Mia already knows about how I feel about Paul's and my relationship, so I went straight to the point and asked her if I should break up with him. Mia said that her mom always tells her to "Follow your heart." Then she added that if I were miserable in the relationship, it was unfair to both Paul and me to continue it.

Right then and there, I decided to end it with Paul. I told Mia how much I valued her friendship and to have a great time with Luke—and I meant it. And I told her I would text Paul to call me when he got up. He called around noon and started raving about the great football games on that night and after he did that for about five minutes, I said I had something to say. He said "What was it?" and I said that I was breaking up with him, that—and I decided to take the high road—that we didn't have much in common (I easily could have said nothing in common) and he needed to be with a girl who shared his interests. I figured he would argue with me about breaking up with him and try to talk me out of it, but he got short and snippy with me, and all he said was "Fine, I've got tons of girls hitting on me all the time," and he hung up and that was that.

Chapter Eleven: Marcus

When I got home from school Friday, Dad said he had gone online to check the school's Parent Portal and he saw that all my grade averages for the first week were an *A* except for a high *B* in English. He said that was "very satisfactory" and a "good start" and how would I like to have "a guy's night out" at the football game. He said I could drive to get some more of my hours in, but that once we got to the game, I could go sit with my friends and then we could meet up afterwards and I could have the experience of driving some at night, which I haven't done yet. At first, I thought that it would be great to go hang out with some of my buds, but then I thought most of my friends are on the football team and I'm still trying to take it slow with Kylee, and, well, maybe it would be good to spend some time with Dad and talk football while we were watching the game. I said I would rather sit with him, and I could tell that he was pleased that I said that.

Driving wise, everything went fine on the way to the game, except for a couple of times I saw Dad gritting his teeth and pressing his right foot into the floorboard when I went over the speed limit by about five mph. Everybody goes five mph over all the time… what was the big deal! I started to say something like that, but since I've been trying to show more maturity—and to especially show my parents that I'm more mature—I decided to keep my mouth shut. I hate to admit that one of my biggest problems last year was not being able to just keep my mouth shut. I'm starting to learn that I can avoid a whole lot of problems later by not saying the first thing that pops into my head.

When we got to the game, Dad and I went up high in the stands so we could get a good seat. It was really hard not being out on the football field Friday night and catching touchdown passes from Caleb during a home game, but Dad knows a whole lot about football so I thought I'd pick his brain about plays and receiver routes and that type of thing. In the first quarter, Paul got flagged for holding, and I started complaining about the poor officiating and Dad said that it wasn't Paul or the officials at blame. He said that Nathan, the guy who is temporarily taking over my wide receiver spot, couldn't shake free from the cornerback, which resulted in Paul having to block his man for so long that he got flagged. The very next play, Caleb got sacked. I had had my eyes locked on Nathan and the corner the entire time, and Nathan never got any separation whatsoever his whole route.

I started complaining about how Nathan was running his routes, that even though he was a freshman, he should be doing a better job. Then Dad got up in my face and said that was one more thing I needed to stop doing—criticizing my teammates. That when I wasn't happy about their performance I should keep my mouth shut. Plus, he said, Nathan was the third receiver, not one of the two regular starters, and if I hadn't messed up by cheating in history class, then Nathan wouldn't have been put in the position of having to play against a first team cornerback, instead he would be trying to shake free from the nickel back when playing on sure passing downs.

Then Dad said something that really stung. "How would you feel right now," he said, "if you heard some of the players blaming you for hurting the team's offensive performance because you were suspended."

Dad was right, and once again, I learned another lesson

about the virtue of keeping my mouth shut. I then tried to get in good with Dad again by saying that I was glad he hadn't contacted Coach Dell when I got suspended from the team for two games and didn't try to talk him out of it, and what Dad said next really surprised me.

"But I did contact him," he said. "I told him I approved of him suspending you 100 percent and then I thanked him for trying to help make you a better person."

This gave me something else to think about. I thought we would do better after the first quarter, because we were playing a team that we had beaten by two touchdowns last year. Instead things got worse. I noticed that Caleb stopped looking Nathan's way at all, which made the other team start to double team Jonathan, the other wide receiver, every time we were in an obvious passing play. And because the passing game fell apart, the linebackers started playing close to the line of scrimmage which resulted in our running game never getting started.

By the end of the first quarter, we were down 7-0 and by halftime, it was 10 to nothing. The final score was 10-6; we only crossed midfield three times the whole game. Dad didn't have to state the obvious. We lost to an inferior team because I had messed up in school—the loss was all my fault. I'm going to have to make it up to the guys and coaching staff when I get back. There's still time for me to put together some good receiving numbers and impress college scouts.

The drive home did not go well. When I first started to pull out of the stadium parking lot and onto the highway, it seemed like the car lights coming toward me were going 100 mph. So I hit the brakes and then some idiot behind me honked his horn and Dad yelled that I had "stopped in the middle of the road" and to either pull over or go forward or do something immediately. Then I panicked and started to pull over to the right but I had hit the left turn signal and the guy behind me really laid into his horn, and I slammed on the brakes again. I was so shaken up that I almost asked Dad to drive home.

Then Dad said to relax, look around and see if it was clear in both directions, then pull out onto the highway. I did look around and things were clear, so out I went. I drove, like, 10 mph below the speed limit all the way home, and, boy, was I glad to pull into our driveway.

Chapter Twelve: Mia

Saturday, when I met Luke for our date, I could tell as soon as I saw him that something was wrong. I didn't find out until we got to where we were going to hike, the national forest, (I thought he was taking me there) that he broke down and told me that his mom has cancer. I comforted him as best as I could and told him he should go live with his granddaddy on weekends, which is what he thought he would try to do. We were holding each other, and I was trying so hard to make him feel that I cared about him, and then he looked at me, and I looked at him, and we kissed for the first time. It was so natural and beautiful…and wonderful. I care about him, and I know he knows that and he cares about me.

Luke then told me that we were going to not dwell on his mom's health and his dad's drinking and this was our day, and we were going to enjoy being together and being out in the outdoors. So we took off hiking up a mountain. Luke kept chattering the whole time, identifying species of birds by the sounds they were making, telling me what trees we were walking under and what their nuts or berries looked like and whether they were edible, and several times he saw wild animal poop or tracks on the ground, and he told me which animals had left it behind—he called the animal sign *spoor*. All this from a boy who got a *D* in biology last year. He told me that he had learned most of this stuff from field guides on birds, mammals, and trees that his granddaddy had given him for Christmas over the years.

Luke is a lot smarter than most people believe. I think because he doesn't wear eye-catching clothes is one reason; another is because it wasn't until the second semester last year that he started talking a little in class and answering questions. Then another thing caught my attention; he was wearing the same shirt he wore on Friday, and I thought back about what he usually wears, and it's the same three or four shirts to school every week. Is that all he has? I bet it is. Of course, my sisters wear all my old clothes; they rarely get anything new, so I'm lucky that Mama sometimes sews me a new blouse.

We had hiked up the mountain for about a half hour and Luke stopped and told me he had to get his bearings. He walked another 10 yards or so, then we went off the trail and into a cove (he called it a hollow) and there were all these wild blackberries. He said, "Here's our dessert." He whipped out a plastic bag and told me to help him pick and while we were doing so, Luke talked about what a healthy food blackberries are and how high they are in Vitamin C. When we were done picking, we hiked for another half hour and we came to this rock outcropping looking down into the valley, and he said we had "reached our destination."

I spread out a blanket to make a sort of picnic table and got out the *arroz con pollo* and deviled eggs and put the food on paper plates and also sliced some carrots and tomatoes from our garden. Meanwhile, Luke scooped out some blackberries with sugar and put that on the plates. It was all so special and sweet and romantic. I had brought two servings of *arroz con pollo* for him because I know he hasn't been getting enough to eat, and Luke ate every bit of what I served him, which made me feel really happy and satisfied with myself. He kept saying over and over how good it was. And he knows now that I can cook, too, which is important to me.

I had never eaten wild berries before, but I trusted him… that he knew what we were gathering was safe to eat. The blackberries were a little tart, but they tasted really good and Luke said some people like to eat them in pies and cobblers. So I asked him if we could stop on the way down the mountain and visit the blackberry patch again and pick some more, and, if we could, I would bake a pie for him. He was all over that suggestion, and I told him I would make one on Sunday and bring him a slice for first period every day next week. He was really excited about that.

I feel so safe and secure every time I am with Luke. He treats me with respect. We were way out in the middle of nowhere, and I wasn't afraid because he was with me. On the way down the mountain, we held hands almost the entire way, and we just talked about everything. I told him I was really thinking about becoming a doctor, and he told me that I would be great at that and he encouraged me to try to be one. I asked him what he thought he might want to do, and he said he was still unsure.

I told him I thought he would make a great high school biology teacher, and he laughed really hard at my suggestion. But then he got quiet for a while, and I could tell that he was thinking about that. "You know," he said, "that might not be a bad idea."

When we got back to our bikes, I was so hoping that he would kiss me again and he took me in his arms and hugged me and gave me another kiss and simply said, "Thank you for having confidence in me."

That moment and that day was one of nicest times of my whole life. We rode our bikes together for about two miles then split up. I met him again at 5 that afternoon at one of our clients for him to mow and trim and for me to babysit. All we had time to do was wave at each other before we both had to get to work, but it was a joy just to see him for that little bit.

A
Month Later

Chapter Thirteen: Luke

When I got home from school Monday and from having spent the weekend at Granddaddy's house, Dad was sprawled out drunk in his easy chair in front of the TV. There were his two best friends nearby: Mr. Bud and Mr. Jack. Mr. Bud comes in a can and Mr. Jack comes in a bottle in case you aren't acquainted with these fine gentlemen. That's normal these days, but what wasn't normal was that there was a strange woman in the house—a nurse. The woman could tell I was confused, and she said her name was Ms. Richards or Richardson or something (I don't know) and she was with hospice. I had heard the word before and I knew it has something to do with somebody taking care of somebody who is going to die before too long. It was then that I was glad to have figured out last month that Mom has cancer, so that I've been able to slowly get used to the idea that she's not going to be around forever, but I had no idea that I was going to lose her this soon.

It was about this time that Dad came out of his drunken stupor, saw me, and growled that I "need to get started right now with vacuuming and washing the new car" he had bought earlier that day. He was so angry that I shouldn't have disagreed with him, but I had to tell him I had to be down the street in 15 minutes to mow two lawns before dark and then I would be back and take care of his car after dark, which is when I usually work on them and he knows that. I turned my back to him to talk to the nurse; I wanted to ask her how Mom was doing.

While I had my back turned, Dad came at me from behind and jerked me around and slapped me hard in the face, yelling, "No, you're going to do it right now!" I went sprawling into the sofa, right in front of the nurse, and I looked up and saw this horrified look on her face, and she started to say something, but I think she was too scared of Dad to say anything.

From down on the floor, I said, "Yes sir, right now, I'm starting," and he acted like he was going to hit me again, but, instead, he slumped back into his chair. I headed out the door, (without talking to the nurse) but I didn't go to our garage... I went to get my bike to ride down the street. My first thought was just to get a little distance between Dad and me, but then I calmed down a little and decided he was probably too drunk to remember the whole thing. And I had to mow those lawns because I couldn't be cutting grass in somebody's backyard after 10:00, but I could be working on a car in the garage after dark. Dad would hopefully be gone somewhere by the time I got home or maybe he would have even gone to the plant to work third shift since he usually leaves around 8:30. Then I came up with the idea that since the two houses weren't that far away, I would walk to them, do my work, and sort of sneak through people's backyards on the way home and when I got near here, figure out if he had left for work yet by whether his car was still here or not.

It was a good plan because by the time I got home, Dad was gone and so was the nurse, and I finished up the new car (it wasn't really a new car, it was just another one of Dad's "bargain" clunkers) a little after 10:30. Then it was time for dinner and Geometry and Spanish I homework, and the fridge was its usual empty self, but I found a can of peaches and another of corn in the pantry and had myself a feast... yeah, right.

I've got an *F* in Geometry (better known as Geometry for Dummies), which is no surprise, so I decided not to do my math homework. It would have taken who knows how long to have figured out what I was supposed to have done, and then I would have done it wrong anyway. I've got a *C* in Spanish, thanks to Mia's help, and I've been learning the vocabulary words really easily but the grammar and pronunciation rules are impossible to learn and boring as all get out. I finished the Spanish homework around 11:30 and went to bed.

The next morning I woke up around 4:00 with this fear that maybe Dad hadn't been too drunk to remember that I had disobeyed him the day before, and what if he were angry about the washing and vacuuming that I had done—as he often is. He's never hit me that hard before, but he's never had a dying wife before and he hasn't been drinking this hard in a long, long time. So I got up, got two energy bars, one for breakfast and the other for lunch, and decided I had better go over that car one more time and see if I had missed anything. It was about 5:15 when I finished eating and going back over the car and all that, and Dad leaves work at 5 and he usually comes straight home because there aren't any car lots or bars open then.

I decided to head for school so I could avoid him altogether that morning, and if I walked instead of ran, I would get there around 6:45 and the doors open at 7:00. There's always some kids hanging around the school doors at 7:00. Do their parents drop them off that early because the kids need some tutoring or the parent has to get to work early? Or are those kids like me... running from somebody or trying to avoid somebody and they've got nowhere else to go. I don't want to know if there are other kids like me. I can't take much more of this.

Chapter Fourteen: Elly

I think lately I've finally started to get my life together. The last four Saturday mornings, I've volunteered to tutor at risk kids at a help center. Ms. Whitney, my guidance counselor at school, set up the whole thing when I went to her and asked if she could find me a volunteer job that has to do with teaching, and it's been great. The kids are between five and eight, and there are other teenage girls there like me helping out. The center's administrator asked me what skill I was best at, whether it was reading, math, arts and crafts… those sorts of things, and I said reading. So I read stories to the really little kids, and then helped the older kids with their pronouncing and vocabulary skills when we read aloud. In the three hours I'm there, I work with six different groups for about 30 minutes at a time.

The first time I was there, the kids were really shy toward me, and I had trouble learning their names and their skill levels. But by the second time, they were more relaxed around me and seemed really glad to see me. And I sort of fell into this groove of how to approach the day's story lesson. On Friday nights, I really enjoy reading the stories the administrator has selected for me and planning out how to approach each group. The whole experience has made me feel wonderful, that I'm doing something meaningful with my life, instead of obsessing over the things that I usually obsess over. More and more, I can see myself teaching maybe third or fourth grade or maybe any elementary grade and really, really enjoying it. The volunteer job will only last about a month, but it will help introduce me to what teaching is like.

The past month, I've also been going to work out with Mom at our club three or four mornings a week before school. I went to Mom and said I wanted to lose some weight, and she said she probably needed to lose a pound or two, and why didn't we start going to the club together before school and work out—that our membership paid for this sort of thing anyway and why not use it. At first, I was dreading the thought of getting up that early, but then I thought about those four pounds I put on over the summer and that made me decide to make the effort.

I've also decided to stop snacking all the time, especially at night when I'm doing my homework or reading. Already, I've lost six pounds, and if I could lose another 18 over the next three or four months, well, that would be awesome. My jeans and skirts are starting to feel looser, and I feel like I look better.

When I was thinking about making all these changes, I also decided to talk to Paige, Mary, and Mia one day at lunch about whether or not I should grow my hair longer. Usually, they disagree when I bring up some sort of question like that, but this time the verdict was unanimous—grow it longer. I started worrying out loud about how frizzy my hair often is and Mary sang out, "Embrace the frizz," and everybody laughed and agreed that my naturally curly hair would look super longer. So far, my hair is maybe just an inch or two longer, but I'm already starting to like my new look.

I don't miss going out with Paul at all, and I definitely don't mind, at least for right now, about not having a boyfriend. A few times, it's been a little awkward passing Paul in the hall, but we don't have any classes together with my being a sophomore and him being a senior. Besides, I've seen him "talking" with a junior in the cafeteria, and Mary said she thinks they're about to become a couple. Good for him. I hope she enjoys sitting on cold bleachers on Friday nights and her heart races to the thrills of watching college football and playing video games on Saturday nights.

Oh, lately, I've had this junior guy, Jonathan, showing me some interest. I only have him in one class, Spanish II, but he's been making a point to come by my table at lunch and ask questions about Spanish verbs or something like that, and he told me he was struggling in Spanish a little and could he text me at night about the homework we had for the next day. The first few texts were just about Spanish, but more and more, they've been about other things, like what do I enjoy doing and what's going on with my life. Boys don't seem to know how to communicate well; they are just so awkward when it comes to that.

Jonathan is on the football team, but he is something called a *receiver*, which apparently means that he doesn't have "to bulk up" all the time like Paul said he was always having to do—so there's that in Jonathan's favor. That makes sense, because Jonathan does not have a big gut like Paul has. So we'll see how things go with him.

And one more thing. Every time Mom and I go to the club, she's letting me drive. In the beginning, I was a little worried about driving in the dark, and I had to take it really slow; the first time I was driving, like, about 10mph under the speed limit, 25 in a 35 mph zone. I know some of the people behind us must have been giving me some dirty looks, but Mom said not to worry about it. She said I had done a nice job with driving when we practiced after school and on weekends, and it was time for me to take the next step.

Then she told me a secret. That Dad had said he thought I could have her car when it was time for me to get my license, that hers was four years old now, and it was time for her to "probably get a new one." She said this whole car situation could be a win-win for the both of us. Yes, indeed, it could-things are looking up for me.

Chapter Fifteen: Marcus

It felt so good to be back playing football after my two-game suspension ended. The team lost both games while I was out, and we lost my first game back (Caleb and me just couldn't seem to get on the same page all night) but we won last Friday night...so I think we're (the team and Caleb and me) going to start clicking from now on. I caught two touchdown passes from Caleb, and the offensive line protected him well all night, which gave me plenty of time to get open. The play that changed the game was a 57-yard catch and run where I caught about a 15-yard pass after creating separation from the corner, then juked the safety, and the next thing that happened was I was slamming the ball in the end zone. It felt amazing, and the home crowd just went absolutely wild. I looked up in the stands where Kylee usually sits and she was cheering like crazy—that was really good to see, too.

Monday morning before first period English 10 Honors, Kylee came up to me and said I "played an awesome game Friday night." I had been thinking about asking her out, but wasn't quite ready to do it, but she's so hot and Homecoming is soon... somebody is bound to hit on her if I waited much longer. So I decided right then on the spur of the moment to ask if she would like to go do something on Saturday night. And she said yes!

I had rather not double date with Joshua and Jordan, but, on the other hand, I can't see Dad or Mom riding in the front seat with me because I can only drive with a licensed adult.

Meanwhile, I'm trying to carry on a conversation with Kylee in the backseat. How uncool is that. It would be just as embarrassing for Kylee and me sitting in the backseat and one of our parents taking us somewhere. I won't have my driver's license until February, and I'm tired of waiting for it, but there's nothing I can do about that… it's so frustrating.

Then I thought that since I'm trying to do things differently this year, since everything I did last year seemed to blow up in my face when I made decisions on my own, especially about girls, I decided to go visit Kylee during lunchtime and asked her where would she like to go Saturday night and given the fact that neither one of us has licenses, how were we going to get wherever we went? In the past, I've always made all those decisions without asking my dates.

Kylee said she had rather not double date with my brother and Jordan, and I quickly agreed about that because I know Jordan can't stand me. Then Kylee said that since last year, we were always going somewhere with somebody from my family driving, she would ask her mom if she would take us to the mall, and we could eat somewhere kind of simple and just walk around and visit stores and shop and talk. I wasn't exactly thrilled about going shopping with Kylee (I mean, what guy would be supercharged about that), but then I thought there are worst things in life than watching a sexy girl try on short skirts and asking for my opinion on how she looks. I can deal with that. I've got one last chance with her; I had better not screw things up this time. So I said I liked her whole plan.

Saturday night, Kylee's mom picked me up around 6:00, and I asked Kylee what she thought about eating at Olive Garden. She said that would be awesome, so that's where we went. We talked about school stuff for a while, and I was really trying to make sure that I didn't control the conversation and tried to ask her what she thought about things. Last year she complained about that toward the end of our relationship. She asked me if I was still planning on playing both pro football and basketball, and I told her no, that I now realized it would be impossible to play both... that I would just have to wait and see which pro sport I picked deciding on how I played in college.

Then she said something that made me mad.

"What happens," she said, "if the pro sports thing doesn't work out at all, what are you going to do then... or suppose if you get injured in high school or college and that's the end of sports?"

I told her that I would likely want to go into broadcasting and be on ESPN or one of the other networks and she replied that those jobs were as hard to get as pro sports jobs and what would I do if that didn't work out. "Would you be willing," she said, "to start at some local TV sports show to build up a resume?"

I started to tell her I wasn't interested in working for some Podunk station out in the middle of nowhere, but I didn't want to get into a fight with her because things had been going so well. Then I started to think that she was probably right about me having to start somewhere small, so I told her that, and she replied that I needed to begin to take some business classes at school in order how to learn how to market myself.

Again, I got mad and tried not to show it, so I told her she was probably right. The more I thought about it, though, the more I realized she was right and later I told her she was which made her smile. She also made me smile when she kissed me goodnight when her mom dropped me off at my house. I had been all twisted up in knots on whether she would want me to kiss her or whether I should try to kiss her, since it had been so long since we had. Then I said, "See you next Saturday night?" and she grinned and said yes, and I kissed her again.

Chapter Sixteen: Mia

When I got to school about 30 minutes before first period, as usual I went to Ms. Hawk's class to make sure I was organized for the day and to talk with Luke about our jobs for the week. As I was walking into the room, I saw that Luke was asleep with his head on top of an open geometry book. There weren't any other students around and Ms. Hawk motioned me up to her desk.

"When I got to school this morning around 7:15," she said, "I saw Luke sitting outside my room and working on his geometry. The first thing I noticed is that there's a big red welt on his face. Luke's not a fighter, do you know how that mark got there?"

I got scared when I heard that because I feared that the only way something like that had happened was because Luke's dad had hit him. Then I started to think would it be good or bad for Luke if Ms. Hawk knew that his dad had probably struck him. Would she report that to social services and would somebody come to Luke's house and investigate if child abuse had happened? What would happen if that happened? Would Luke's dad get really angry and really light into him then? Would my talking to Ms. Hawk make things worse for him?

A minute or so must have gone by, and I still hadn't answered Ms. Hawk, and all I could think to say was "I haven't seen Luke since Saturday when we went canoeing for our date," which wasn't answering her question at all.

"Sweetie," she said. "I figured you two were dating by now. I saw that coming last year. You haven't answered my question."

"Luke's mom is dying, his dad is drinking hard, and Luke is scared of his father," I blurted out. Then I teared up. I tried not to, but it happened anyway. I don't like to lose control of my emotions. I was so glad that nobody else was in the room.

"Luke is so sweet to me," I said and then the tears started to rain down, and all these thoughts rushed into my mind. We've had four dates now and they've all been awesome. On our second one, we went hiking into the mountains and Luke showed me how to fly fish for wild trout, and I caught my first fish. I never squeal, but I shrieked when I got that trout (Luke called it a *brookie*) up on the bank. It was flopping all over the place. Luke caught three, and he showed me how to clean them. From cooking with Mama, I know how to clean fish, but he was so patient and passionate about how to tell me how to get them ready to cook that I didn't want to interrupt him. Earlier, I had asked him what would we eat if we couldn't catch any fish. He just gave me this confident smile and said, "Don't you worry about that. We'll catch 'em."

He made a fire right next to the creek, and he cooked the trout for lunch along with some mushrooms and sweet onions he had asked me to bring from home. He was so confident and he was so like a man the whole time he was talking and explaining things to me and preparing the trout. The fish were so good to eat. Earlier, I had made some churros, and I brought them for our dessert, and he really liked them and praised my cooking skills. I felt so special.

On our third date, we went biking out into the country and had a picnic lunch. Since he had been in charge of the entrée the Saturday before, it was my turn to bring the main course. I brought cilantro corn cakes, and Luke ate so many that I wished I had brought more from home. This past

Saturday, we went canoeing down the river that flows through town. Luke and I bartered with the canoe livery's owner, telling him that Luke would mow his lawn at home and at the livery and I would give the office a really good cleaning in exchange for the man letting us rent a canoe.

We ate lunch on an island where we stopped to make a fire. This time, I knew not to worry about him catching fish. He caught four really big what he called smallmouth bass, but he said we weren't going to eat them because they were such a special fish. It was important to let them go so that they could grow even bigger.

Later, we beached the canoe on an island and went wading into the river. Luke showed me how to cast by standing behind me and sort of guiding my arms in the correct casting motion. I never would have thought fishing could be romantic, but it was... with him. I felt so close to him while he was touching my arms that I turned around and kissed him. He teased me and said I needed to be a good student and to stop fooling around with the teacher.

Next, Luke tied to the line what he called a *crankbait* (it's like this hard plastic minnow looking creature that sort of wiggles through the water) and said I was going to catch five or six sunfish with the lure thingy and we would have them for lunch. I didn't believe him, but I did catch those fish, I really did. Can you believe that, I caught our whole lunch!

Ms. Hawk started patting me on the shoulder which snapped me back into reality, and I finally stopped crying and I at last told her what I had been fearing, that Luke's dad might hit him worse if somebody from social services came to the house and investigated what was going on. Ms. Hawk got this worried look on her face when I told her that and she stuttered something. I couldn't hear what it was.

About that time, other students started coming into the room, and I went to wake Luke up and try to help him a little bit with his geometry homework before English class started. As I had feared, he only had done three of his equations for homework, and, of course, with Luke's horrible math skills, they were all wrong. How could anybody have so much potential in English and biology and be so bad in math? I guess I find something like that hard to understand because school has always been so easy for me.

In third period Ecology, the secretary called over the intercom for Luke to go to guidance. I figured something terrible must have happened because Luke didn't come back to class and wasn't in Yearbook seventh period. He called me that night to tell me that his mom had died that morning.

Homecoming

Chapter Seventeen: Luke

It's been hard since Mom died last month. I miss her. After she died, Dad took a week off work and stayed drunk almost the entire time. If Mia hadn't been bringing me something to eat every school morning and if I wasn't able to keep going to Granddaddy's house every weekend, I don't think I could have stood it with Dad screaming and cursing at me all the time. I was so hungry all the time, too.

But all that's behind me now. Two weeks ago, Dad and I got into a really big argument when I got home from school one afternoon. He had sobered up enough to be working on one of his cars before he went to work at the plant, and he yelled at me to come over. "What's this I hear about you and some Mexican girl," he said. (He didn't use the words *Mexican* or *girl*, but I'm not going to repeat what he said.) "My boss," Dad went on, "said he hired the two of you to mow his lawn and work in his garden, and you two were awful 'friendly' with each other."

I was terrified when he said that, and I didn't know what to say back. If I denied that Mia and I were dating, he probably would hit me, and if I admitted that she was my girlfriend, he would hit me. If I told him, it was none of his business, he would definitely hit me for being smart with him. I hesitated for what seemed like forever and before I could say something, he walked over and slapped me harder than he ever has and yelled, "Answer me, boy!"

I confessed that Mia was my girlfriend and that we ran a lawn and gardening business together and that's what I was doing after school and on weekends. He then ordered me to break up with that girl (again, I'm not going to repeat what he really said).

Dad said that this weekend, a friend of his was going to drop us off at a car lot, and he and I both were going to drive cars back home for me to clean up. I told him that I only had a learners permit, and it would be illegal for me to drive by myself yet, and he cursed at me and said, "Do as you're told." I quickly said "Yes, sir." I didn't want to get hit again. I'm not going to break up with Mia. I'm not going to drive a car by myself without having my license. If the police stopped me on the way home, I'd get a criminal record and I'm not even 16.

My face was hurting so bad from where he hit me, and already I could feel my left eye going shut. I had hoped to go bow hunting that afternoon behind Elly's house; her dad had again given me permission to hunt there. But with my eye the way it was, I was afraid I wouldn't be able to shoot straight enough to kill a deer. I had been looking forward to going hunting for so long because with fall here, the lawn mowing business is finally slowing down and I actually have time to have some fun in the evenings.

I went to lie in my bed and then I decided that I just couldn't take it anymore, that I wasn't going to live like this anymore. While Dad was still outside, I packed all my camouflage clothes for deer hunting and my fishing lures and flies and fold-up fly rod in my hunting day pack. I wasn't leaving that stuff behind no matter what because I was going to run away to Granddaddy's house as soon as Dad went to work around 8:30.

When Dad finally left for work, I wrote a note saying that I was going to live at Granddaddy's house and left it on the kitchen table. Then I got my pack and got on my bike and took off. I knocked on Granddaddy's door around 9:15 and when he opened it, I started crying and blurted out everything that had been happening with Dad and his drinking and hitting me, and I even told him about Mia and me and that her family had come from Mexico and he knew how Dad felt about Mexicans. Granddaddy looked so sad and then he told me that "Of course, you can live here, Luke."

Then he told me something that I didn't know about.

"Do you ever wonder why you don't have a grandmother?" he asked. "It's because she left me many years ago because of my drinking. Your father can't hold his liquor and I couldn't either. Luke, promise me you'll never start drinking."

I promised him that I wouldn't, and I meant it. After all, I had promised Mom years ago that I never would. Anyway, why would I want to be like Dad in any possible way.

Then, Granddaddy asked me about my grades in school and what was Mia like. I told him I had my best ever report card the first nine weeks. I made an *A* in English and Yearbook, a *B* in World History II and Ecology, a high *C* in Phys Ed because of the stupid health stuff, a *D* in Spanish, and an *F* in Geometry. The grade in Spanish really bothered Mia (I told Granddaddy all about her and how smart she is) so we've been working more on Spanish than Geometry during her tutoring on Tuesdays and Thursdays. I told him that Mia said I can make a *C* in Spanish the next nine weeks, and I think I can. I didn't tell him that probably 90 percent of the kids in Geometry fail—the whole class is a circus with students misbehaving and texting or listening to music (some of them don't even bother to put in their earbuds) the whole period.

Granddaddy then said something that caused me to get the best night's sleep I've had in a long, long time. "I'll change the locks so that your dad can't ever get into my house, and tomorrow night while your dad's at work, we'll go get the rest of your things." He paused for a little while and added the best part, "Oh, by the way. If I were you, I'd hang onto Mia. She sounds like a keeper."

I think I finally have a home again.

Chapter Eighteen: Elly

About two weeks before Homecoming, Jonathan asked me out for it, and I said yes. The way he did wasn't very romantic. He just sent me a text saying, "Hey, ya wanna go to Hoco with me???" I mean, really, three questions marks and not calling me in person—that's not very mature. But I do sort of like him and we have been talking and I have been worrying that no other guy would ask me out this whole year. I know I should have more self-confidence than that, and I have been feeling better about my appearance.

I've lost 12 pounds now since I started my diet, and Mom and I started working out at our family's club. My hair is about three inches longer, too, since I started letting it grow out, and—this was pretty daring for me—but since I've gone down a dress size, Mom and I went shopping and we bought two skirts that show just a hint of my knees. I don't feel my legs are so chubby anymore. I guess I don't look half bad.

Mom and I went shopping for Homecoming, and we bought this gorgeous dress. We decided to go with a hi-low dress that has a sleeveless lacy top, a sweetheart neckline, and a floral print flare skirt. Mom wanted me to wear my hair up, but that's what I would have done in the past when my hair was shorter, so I wanted to wear it down. Besides, Paige and Mary both told me to wear it down because Jonathan would like it better that way, and I needed to "show off those longer locks" as Mary said.

When Jonathan picked me up, he gave me a beautiful wrist corsage, which I felt was very sweet of him. Then Jonathan took me out to dinner at this really nice steak and seafood restaurant. He ordered a ribeye steak, and I got the grilled seafood platter because I figured it wouldn't have many calories. When it came time for dessert, I told Jonathan that I was stuffed (even thought I wasn't) and he said that was fine, but he would go ahead and get some cheesecake. I liked the fact that he didn't hound me to eat more like Paul always did, and I told Jonathan that I would enjoy watching him eat his cheesecake.

The food and atmosphere at the restaurant were very nice, and I told that to Jonathan several times as a way of making conversation, but, well, the whole dinner was boring. He just didn't talk much, because I don't think he is... very bright. I mean, I asked him about his grades (I only have him in Spanish II, of course) and he said that he had a *C* in everything and he said he was fine with that. Most of his classes were just the general ones, not like the honors classes he should be taking if he wants to prepare for college. I asked him what he wanted to do after he finished high school, and he simply said, "Something will turn up." I mean, he's a junior, and he's not even thinking about his future. Boys are so immature—when do they start to grow up?

It was the same thing when we went to Homecoming. He was attentive to me; he didn't flirt with other girls, he asked me if I wanted something to drink or eat and offered to go get it...those sorts of things, which were all fine. But I can't remember if we ever talked about anything, because, well, we didn't. Overall, being with Jonathan was just a different kind of boring than being with Paul except when Jonathan kissed me goodnight, it was clear that he had shaved that day. On my 1 to 10 man scale, I would rate Paul as a 3 and Jonathan a 5, better make that a 4. But let me give things a while and see if they get better.

I want a relationship like Mia and Luke have. Every time I see them together they are talking the entire time, especially before class in English and all during Yearbook and when they are walking down the hall. The other day I asked Mia what they talked about all the time, and she said things like current events and school and what their jobs were that week and what did the other one want to go do for their weekly Saturday date and what their futures would be like, "Those sorts of things," she said. I know I've said this before, but sometimes I get so jealous of her and Luke, because I know now that Luke really liked me a lot before Mia came along. But Caleb, by far, is still the boy I want most to notice me.

And he has been lately since I've lost weight and let my hair grow out. Last Tuesday in Ecology class right after Ms. Bradley had stopped teaching for the day, I saw Caleb get up and go to the trashcan and he stopped at my desk on his way back to his. He told me I "had been looking differently lately" and did I enjoy the church dinner the other night; he couldn't be there because of football practice, of course, and getting ready for the "big game." Had I been at the game and seen the three touchdowns he threw? We must have had a conversation for two whole minutes and it was almost as if he were flirting with me (I can only hope) and it was awesome.

Then Caleb left me and poked Luke (who for some weird reason was dressed in his hunting clothes) in the back pretty hard and said, "Hey, camo boy, ya going hunting during lunchtime?" Then Caleb made some remark about how guys like Luke gave the school a bad reputation. I saw Luke's eyes "flash" and his expression harden but he didn't say anything and then just looked away. I next looked at Mia, who like always, was sitting next to Luke, and I could see this look of fury come across her face. I had never seen her look that way, but she didn't say anything either.

At lunch, I asked Mia why was Luke wearing his hunting clothes to school, and she said, "Luke ran away from home last night because his dad's been hitting him, that's all he has to wear right now." I knew that Luke's mom had died recently, but I didn't realize that things were that bad for him. Why was Caleb being so judgmental about how Luke looked, that was wrong of him. Then I realized something else... that Caleb had been bullying Luke in Ecology class and whether or not he knew about Luke's home situation, he shouldn't have been treating Luke like that... no way.

Chapter Nineteen: Marcus

I almost didn't get to take Kylee to Homecoming, but things could have been a lot worse. I guess, looking back, I could have been messed up really bad. Friday night's football game was huge for us. We came in with a record of 3-3, and if we were going to have any chance to make the playoffs, we had to beat Springwood that night. Caleb and me are finally totally clicking and on the first drive of the night, I caught four passes for 33 yards. The last 12 of those were on a fade route into the end zone. Caleb laid the ball into me just perfectly, and the crowd was screaming like crazy when we went up 6-0. Then Coach Dell shocked everyone, including our offense, and told us to stay on the field—he said we were going for a two-point conversion instead of just an extra point. Coach called for me to give one fake at the line and then go for a quick slant over the middle. It worked perfectly and all of a sudden, we're up 8-0. I mean the crowd is just exploding because the local paper had predicted we would lose to Springwood. On Homecoming weekend? On our home field? I don't think so!

In the second quarter, Springwood started to come back and even went ahead by 10-8. But right before the half, we went into our two-minute drill. I think Springwood was expecting Caleb to air it out to me because they were double covering me with a corner and safety on every play. But, instead, Coach Dell started calling all these dump it off plays. Caleb kept hitting Joshua for, like, seven or eight yards for four straight plays. Last year, I would've been angry that I wasn't getting the ball and my big brother was, but I thought I could see what Coach was trying to do—he was trying to make sure that I was going to be eventually left alone with just one defensive back covering me. And I can't be covered one on one—no way, no how.

All of a sudden, we were on Springwood's 40, and there's 25 seconds left. We come to the line of scrimmage, and sure enough, I come up to the line with just one corner on me and Caleb calls an audible. The back tries to jam me at the line, but I'm by him and down the right side in a flash. Caleb hits me at the 30 and I'm into the end zone like two seconds later—totally untouched—and after the extra point, we're up 15-10 at the half.

And really after that, I don't remember much what happened. Springwood got the ball to start the half and it was a good three and out stand by our defense. When we got the ball, there was a holding call on Paul on second down, which eventually turned into a third and 15 situation—and an obvious passing down. I had double coverage with a corner and safety and I just couldn't break free of them, and Caleb tried to squeeze the ball in to me. I must have gotten absolutely creamed by the both of them because the last thing I remember was leaping for the ball and getting hammered from both sides.

When I came to, I saw a doctor and a team trainer looking over me, and I was in the locker room. They told me I had experienced a very mild concussion and that I was through for the night. I felt okay and said I was ready to go back in, but the doctor just smiled and said, "No way."

The next thing I knew, Dad was in the locker room, and he and the doctor and trainer talked and they decided that I should spend the night at the hospital, just as a precaution. I was a little groggy, and I didn't find out until the next morning that we had lost 20 to 15. It's going to be really hard to make the playoffs now, and that was when I was really hoping to show my stuff for college scouts.

The good news was that I did get to go to Homecoming the next night. Kylee and I double dated with Joshua and Jordan. It was the first time that I can ever remember Jordan being nice to me. She didn't glower at me all night—not even once. We had a really nice dinner; I don't remember what I had but it was good. Kylee and I only danced maybe two or three times all night, but we did sit and talk a lot and actually that was kind of nice. She told me that she made the All-A honor roll, and I've got to confess that I was pretty happy to say that I had made the A-B roll the first nine weeks. She talked about wanting to run her own business or do something with a human service agency, and she talked a lot about how those type jobs would be very satisfying. I've been actually listening to her, and I can tell she appreciates that.

I had to go back to the doctor on Sunday and Monday, and on Tuesday, both the doctor, our trainer, and my parents decided that it would be best if I sat out this coming Friday's game. That means I will already have missed three of the first seven games of the season. But there was nothing I could do about it. Even Kylee told me that sitting out was the best thing for me, and she said I could root the team on from the bench, and she would be waiting for me after the game—that maybe we could get a bite to eat with Joshua and Jordan. I really appreciate how Kylee has been acting toward me, and I'll be ready for that next game in two weeks.

Chapter Twenty: Mia

I was so shocked the other day when Leigh and I were named as the two sophomores on the Homecoming court. Leigh, I can understand, she's absolutely beautiful, she does well in school, and she's a cheerleader and very popular. But, honestly, I've never even thought about something like that happening to me. I really never have cared about those types of things; they just seem so unimportant and temporary compared to the things I really want out of life. Still, it was an honor that the students in my grade would vote for me.

My family and I were at dinner on the Monday night before Homecoming, and I finally decided I had better let Poppa and Mama know about the nomination because he was going to have to escort me onto the field at halftime Friday night. Poppa said he was really proud of me and said he knew a guy in our neighborhood, Henrique (he's a junior) that would be just perfect for me, and then went on and on about how he was friends with Henrique's poppa and he could set things up with the man and Henrique for the Saturday night dance. Mama interrupted him and said, "Mia can choose her own boyfriends, she doesn't need our help."

Then Isabella and Emma both started giggling, and Mama and I glared at them and they stopped laughing. I've told them over and over that they are not to tell Poppa about Luke and me, and Mama has warned them they will be punished if they do. Mama said I should have let her know earlier about my nomination and I replied that I knew that, but I was worried about not having anything that nice to wear, and I didn't want them to waste money on buying something for me just for Friday night. I added that I wasn't going to the dance Saturday night.

It's true, I'm not. Luke and I talked about whether to go or not, and I would so much like to be seen with him in front of the other students. I know everybody knows we're a couple. But Luke said he didn't have the right kinds of clothes and he's never danced before, and I could tell that he felt so awkward about the whole thing. It's true, he doesn't have anything to wear that's nice enough.

Finally, we decided what we would do on Saturday night. We've never been out at night together, so Luke suggested that we ride our bikes to the local Dairy Queen and instead of having just an ice cream cone like we did one time when we were ninth graders, we would both order a milkshake and he would pay for both of them. And we could sit and talk for a long time and be together and drink our milkshakes very slowly "to make the evening last," he said.

What he said was so loving and sweet, and I told him that would be perfect. On Friday night, Poppa dressed up with the coat and tie that he wears to mass on Sundays, and I was proud to have him escort me out onto the field. Mama made time to make a new blouse for me; she must have stayed up late for several nights to sew it in secret. I teared up when I found out what she had done, and I told her how much I loved her and appreciated her for everything she does for us. Mama said she was proud of me and was glad that Luke and I were together, but the time was still not right for us to let Poppa know about our relationship. I fear that the time will never be right, but I'm not going to worry about that now.

We went home right after the ceremony, Poppa had to go to bed and get some sleep because he had to get up at 5 the next morning to go to his Saturday janitor's job at the hospital, and

Mama and my sisters and I had to clean the house and chicken run before Luke and I went off to do our Saturday jobs. I wasn't interested in the football game anyway. What Elly has been telling me about football games is true; what's the point of them kicking and throwing that ball all over the place? I brought my World History II book and research notes to the game and worked on the paper I have to do on the Bubonic Plague in Europe during the 1400s and 1500s. It's really fascinating reading.

Saturday night with Luke was so wonderful. He told me I looked as beautiful at night as I did during the day, and we just sat for an hour at the Dairy Queen, talking and holding hands. I'm so glad that Luke is not living with his father anymore, and I can tell that he is more relaxed. I know I won't see any more bruises on his face. It would just tear me up inside when I would see them. I was scared for him.

After we finished our milkshakes, we went walking for several blocks up and down in front of the Dairy Queen. Luke said that his granddaddy said that when he got his driver's permit on March 15, he would take me out to dinner someplace... that we would finally have "a big time date." Luke then said something really unbelievable, that he had never eaten at a "sit down" restaurant before, and he would like to have that experience. I know that his family is poor, just like mine, but it was really the first time that I realized that his family didn't even have the things that we have or done the things we've done.

I told him I didn't care about us going to expensive places, that being with him was all I wanted. Then we kissed for the longest time. I don't care what happened at the Homecoming dance. I'm sure lots of kids had a good time. But I also really, really believe that nobody there had a better time than I did or was with a person so special.

Wheels

Chapter Twenty-One: Luke

When Ms. Hawk started off class on Monday about how we were going to have a discussion on our next topic for a paper, I was excited. I like to write and I think that's what I do best in school. But when she said we were all going to write about our experiences on learning how to drive, I thought of Mom and the last time we really did something together was when she took me driving. That was when she was just starting to get sick, which made me really depressed.

Then I thought about Dad cursing at me the only time or two he did take me driving, and I tried to force those thoughts out of my head. I don't want to think of him... at all. At first when I went to live with Granddaddy, he and I both worried that Dad was going to try to take me back to his house—that's why Granddaddy changed the locks. But Dad never even came by, he didn't even call to see if I was really at his house. I sort of am glad that Dad didn't check on me or call. That means, he and I are done with each other forever, I guess ...I hope.

Ms. Hawk kept calling on people for them to tell about their driving screw-ups. Mary told about the time she saw a dog run across the street in front of her, and Mary tried to slam on the brakes, but instead hit the gas pedal and almost hit the dog. Missing the dog, she ran into a parked car. Everybody laughed at that. Allen said he hit a stone wall in his driveway when he was backing out. Yeah, I saw the dent on his dad's car that he put there.

Paige told about the first time she and her dad went driving together and she was pulled over by a police car. She was driving like 15 in a 35 mph zone, and the cop thought something was wrong with her car. The thing that everybody laughed at was that Paige said she thought she was going really fast and was speeding—Paige said she felt like the car was about to go out of control as it was and the cop wanted her to go faster. Paige said she got so flustered that she had to get out of the driver's seat and let her dad drive her back home.

Granddaddy and I have been driving a lot together in his Ford F-150 that he's had for a long time, and I have been taking the usual class with one of those driving schools guys. I haven't been having any problems. The first time I drove was when I was twelve. Mom and Dad went off to a car race, and Dad told me while they were gone to clean up two cars he had just bought. He had been showing me how to back up one car and then drive the next car into position so that I could reach the hose and later the extension so I could vacuum the second car. So I was pretty comfortable with the whole backing up and driving up thing, and when I got into the second car, I just decided to take it on a spin around the block. It was early on a Sunday morning and nobody was out, so I decided to take it on a couple more spins around a few more blocks. No big deal. Ever since, I've been really comfortable driving a car, except when Dad was with me and yelling his lungs out. I know now that I shouldn't have been driving so young. I was just a kid then.

But the closer Ms. Hawk got to calling on me, the more nervous I got. I was afraid I would tear up if I had to talk about Mom and me driving, and I didn't want to talk about Dad and me doing anything and I sure as heck didn't want to talk about breaking the law driving when I was younger. And I got like this panic attack, and when Ms. Hawk called on Mia and I knew she was going to call on me next, I raised my hand and said I needed to go to the nurse. Or did I ask to go to guidance?

Anyway, I got permission to leave the room and went to guidance to talk to Ms. Whitney, my guidance counselor, but she had like this long line of kids waiting to see her. From the looks on their faces, they were all having a bad morning just like I was. Why can't the school have more guidance counselors, doesn't somebody, can't somebody realize a lot of us are in pain?

I waited in line for about 10 minutes, and the line was just as long when I decided to leave as it was when I got there. By that time, I had gotten my nerves under control and had tried to force my sad thoughts about Mom and my angry thoughts about Dad out of my head. I also figured that Ms. Hawk had finished going around the room by then anyway.

I got the guidance secretary to sign a note sending me back to class, and I got another panic attack when I couldn't remember if I was supposed to have been at the nurse or guidance? When I got back in the room and gave Ms. Hawk the note, she said to see her after class. Yep, she must have thought I lied to her, but I really didn't. I just wanted out of the room for a second.

When I went to her after class, she didn't even ask about the note. She asked if I wanted to write about something other than driving, and I said, "Oh, gosh, yes." She sort of laughed at that and said, "Why don't you write about the time last year when you killed your first deer?" She remembered me telling her about that when I was in her ninth grade class. I told her that would be freaking awesome, but I didn't use the word freaking of course. Anyway, that's what I'm going to write about. I've already figured out the title, "The Time Granddaddy and I Went Deer Hunting."

Chapter Twenty-Two: Elly

Sunday after church, Mom and I decided to go driving out in the country. Dad and my brothers were watching football, which Mom and I think is just about the most boring sport ever, so she said, "Let's get out of here," and I was all over that. She said she wanted me to get some practice driving faster because the fastest I've ever gone is 35 around town.

Once we got outside the city limits, the speed limit went up to 55, but Mom said I didn't have to drive that fast right away, especially if I wasn't comfortable doing it. When I finally got Mom's car up to 45, it just felt like I was going way too fast and it was a little scary. Like, what would happen if I sneezed or something or some cow was in the road or a deer ran across. I could lose control of the whole thing. So I went back down to 40 and felt better about the speed thing. People kept coming up on my back bumper which made me really nervous, and one man was so rude that he honked at me like three times in a second. Mom said, "Don't pay that jerk any mind, just keep going. You're doing fine." That made me feel better.

Later, I got more and more confident, and before I knew it, I was all the way up to 50! I was feeling pretty cocky about the whole thing, I've got to say. But when I was up that high, one time I took a quick glance over at Mom, and she was like pressing her left foot into the carpet and had this worried look on her face, so I thought I had better back off on the gas a little.

When we got back to town, Mom said, "Let's go shopping at the mall. You've lost more weight, haven't you? So have I, let's buy ourselves some new outfits." It's true, we've lost weight from working out most mornings before school. I'm now down 16 pounds, so I only want to lose eight more and Mom said she's "dropped six." Dad has noticed, too, she said, laughing.

We went looking for skirts, and I put one on that was about two inches above my knees, and I kept looking at Mom to see if she felt it was too short or if she thought my legs were still too big, and she just said, "It looks good on you, let's buy it." And we did. It's the first time since I was like in elementary school that I've worn a skirt or dress this short. I'm feeling a lot better about myself these days.

On our way out of the mall, we passed by this ice cream parlor, and Mom and I were both looking inside at the people eating there and finally she said, "Oh, why not, we need to reward ourselves. We'll work out an extra 15 minutes tomorrow morning." So we went inside and each had a single scoop of chocolate mint chip. We had had so much fun together. While we were eating our ice cream (life is definitely better when you're eating something chocolate), Mom asked me what I thought of Jonathan, and I said he was just "a slight upgrade" over Paul, and our relationship wasn't ever going to amount to anything. She nodded her head at that. I think she's pleased that I don't have a guy that I really like in my life... that I'm not too serious about any guy.

Everything was going just perfect. I felt so close to Mom, and it was so good to have girl time with her... then I had my first accident. We were only about five blocks from our house and driving through the neighborhood next to ours. I was only driving 25 in a 25 mph zone and Mom and I were laughing about something, and I took my eyes off the road for just a second to say something to her and this stupid cat ran right out in front of me. I swerved to miss it and ran right into somebody's mailbox. It all happened so fast. I had been going 50 mph out in the country and hadn't had any problems all day and then I take out somebody's mailbox and go up over the curb and into a front yard a little bit.

Mom and I got out of the car, and we saw that I had put this big bump in the front bumper and there were scratches on it, too, from where I went up over the curb I guess. I started to cry and told Mom that she should back the car back into the street and park it before we knocked on the door to report what I had done. But Mom said, "No, you're going to back the car slowly back into the street and park it yourself, just like you would if I wasn't here. You can do it, I have confidence in you." I got myself together and did just like she said, and then we went to knock on the door.

The man didn't look too happy when he opened the door. He must have seen or heard what I had done from inside. Mom said she wanted to pay him right then for the cost of my totaling his mailbox, and she ended up giving him $75.00 in cash. Later she told me she didn't want Dad asking her what "that check for $75.00 to a strange man was for."

With that man paid, I started worrying what Dad would say when he found out about the car. Mom thought and thought and she said these were the possibilities: We could confess to Dad about "the mailbox affair" and he would yell at both of us. We could pretend that we had no idea how the bump and scratches got on the bumper. We could tell Dad that the bump and scratches got there when we were inside the mall. Or, last, we could just wait and hope that he was too busy at work to notice and when several months passed by and he said something about the scratches, we could say something like, "Oh we told you about that, don't you remember when Elly hit that mailbox?" Finally, we decided to go with option number four. Mom said men don't have very good memories about some things.

Chapter Twenty-Three: Marcus

I haven't had a particularly good week, and it started with Mom and Dad buying me a used Fiat—really, a Fiat, a used Fiat—a three-year-old used Fiat, c'mon. About the only thing worse would have been a minivan. I really think I've done a good job at school and everything else this year—that I've grown up a lot from last year. I made the *A-B* honor roll in high school for the first time. That sure didn't get me much love from them. I mean my parents own a practically new BMW and a Mercedes for their personal use. They bought Joshua a new car—a Ford Mustang—when he got his license. I remember very clearly that they said that would be the car he could take away for college in a couple years. That was why the car had to be new. They've always favored him over me because he's "Mr. Perfect First Male Child."

Mom and me have been driving some with the Fiat. She picked me up after football practice several times last week and let me drive home. Caleb and Paul and some of the other guys on the team saw her do it and have been ragging me about "What's up with the old lady car" type crap. I can't stand it.

The other day Mom said she would let me drive the Fiat to school for some extra practice and then she would go on to work in it. I was so embarrassed to be seen in that piece of junk again that I lied and said I had to get to school early so we left 20 minutes sooner than usual. Backing out of our driveway, I ran over the curb and Mom snapped at me, so I drove right back up over the curb and went into the grass just a little bit and ended up tearing up some of Dad's precious lawn. It had rained big time the night before and Mom yelled at me again to stop and I threw on the brakes. I ground up some more grass when I was trying to get back on the asphalt in our driveway, but the grass was so wet I ended up spinning my wheels and the next thing I knew the Fiat is stuck in a rut in the yard. What a piece of junk.

It was a good thing that Dad had already gone to the office because for sure he would have come running out of the house and yelling at the top of his lungs. I have to admit I was a little shook up at that point—I mean having an accident in your front yard is not a good way to start the day. Mom asked, "Do you want me to take over and get us out of the rut," and I have to admit that I said yes. She said she would call a professional gardener to come fix the lawn today before Dad came home and that she wouldn't tell Dad—that maybe he wouldn't notice. When you have to pin your hopes for a good day on a gardener's skills—well, what can I say?

School didn't go any better when I got there. It was the week we were going to do skills tests in phys ed instead of behind the wheel stuff, and Coach Miley announced that first on the list was running 50-yard dashes. That's my thing and nobody ever beats me in speed tests, either on the football team and, especially, in phys ed. And Luke, Luke of all people, beat me by a tenth of a second. I know I should have won, but I wasn't going full out.

After Luke won, Coach Miley got this wide-eyed, half crazy look and asked Luke if he had ever thought about trying out for cross country or track at the least or if he had maybe thought about trying out for the football team as a cornerback. Luke said he wasn't interested, that he had some kind of job after school. Then Henson asked me if I would like a rematch with Luke in a 50-yard dash, and all the guys started yelling "rematch, rematch." And crap, if Luke didn't beat me again when we ran one-on-one. I mean, he barely edged me out, but the kid can run, I'll give him that.

The next thing I know, Coach Miley is asking Luke if he wants to come to football practice and try a few defensive snaps as a corner. Luke says he's not interested and Miley then, like, bribes him by saying that Luke going to practice could count as his extra credit project in class—the "extra" project we're all supposed to do. Luke agreed to come one day next week because he has probably as much interest in doing that project as I do.

After football practice that day while Joshua was driving me home, I was complaining about Mom and Dad, Joshua having a Mustang, the Fiat thing, the phys ed skills thing, and Luke, and Joshua got mad and pulled over the car. He was just steaming. He told me that I've grown up a lot this year, but that I can still be a "whiner."

"Look," he said. "I earned that Mustang because Mom and Dad gave me a set of expectations: A-B honor roll every nine weeks in 9th and 10th grade, no behavior issues at school or home, and best effort in sports and life. And I met them. Can you say the same? If not, shut up!"

I started to say something, but then I realized he was right—crap, I hate it when he's right. Then he said cornerback was a weak spot on the team and it had been both years I was on the team, that it would be good if we had somebody that could stay with me and challenge me a little. I guess he was right about that, too. After all, he's one of the team captains and he is a leader on the team. I guess I've still got some growing up to do, but I'm not going to admit that to Joshua. We've only got two games left in the season, and we're only at .500 and there will be no playoffs for us this year. We've got to start thinking about getting the best players on the team for next year.

Chapter Twenty-Four: Mia

The other day, Mama and Poppa told me that they don't have the money for me to take a drivers' training course this year, so I won't be getting my license even when I'm old enough. They said that they had been studying and studying how to afford for me to take the class, but there's just not enough money and they're sorry. I knew that might happen. We can only afford one car, that's why my parents have to leave so early for work every day so that Poppa can drop Mama off before he goes to his construction job. Poppa has been letting me drive to Sunday Mass every weekend, but he said we can't afford to take me out after school or on weekends to practice drive because of the high cost of gas. I understand, but I am disappointed.

I felt good that my parents also promised they would do everything possible to save enough money for me to take drivers' training next year. I know they will, they always try to do their best for my sisters and me. I'm just frustrated that I have gotten to drive so little this year. I told Luke how I felt, and the next day he said he had a proposition for me. He said, "How about Granddaddy and me coming over Saturday after your father leaves for his weekend janitor's job. Granddaddy can drop me off, and I'll clean your hen house while you do your other chores. Then when Granddaddy comes back, if your mama says it's alright, you can drive our truck to Granddaddy's house, and I'll fix everybody lunch since you've made so many meals for me."

It was obvious Luke had really thought all this out, and it was so sweet of him. That's one of many reasons why I'm so happy to be his girlfriend. Then he surprised me again. He said he had asked Elly's dad if he could bow hunt from a blind in their backyard, just as he did last year, and her dad had said yes. How would I, Luke said, "like to sit in the blind with him Saturday evening until dark and wait for deer to come into the backyard?" I then asked how would I get home that night, and he suggested that I contact Elly and ask her if I could have a sleepover? I did just that and now I get to spend most of the day with my boyfriend and the night with my best girlfriend. So looking forward to all that really took away the disappointment about the license situation.

Luke was so kind to come over and clean out the chicken coop, and I felt just like a queen waiting for her chariot to depart when it was time to go to Luke's grandfather's house. Of course, Luke couldn't sit in the front with me, but he jokingly said that he was looking forward to me chauffeuring him around. I was a little nervous driving a strange vehicle, especially a Ford pickup, but Luke's granddaddy was so helpful to me that I relaxed really soon.

For lunch, Luke fixed me grilled venison tenderloin from a deer he killed last year, and he also cooked some baked potatoes and asparagus to go with it. His granddaddy said he had to do some things outside so he left us alone at the table together, which was so romantic. I know what Luke's granddaddy was doing and that was kind of him to let Luke and me be together by ourselves and talk. I gave Luke the biggest kiss after lunch and told him how lucky I was to be with him, and then he kissed me too. He said he was the lucky one.

"No more romancing for now," he said then. "Let's go kill a deer." Of course, I don't own any camo clothes, but earlier Luke told me to dress with a black top and a black or brown hat and said that would be all I would need. When his granddaddy dropped us off at Elly's, Luke started spraying me all over with some kind of pine smelling scent and I asked him what on earth that was for. He said it was so the deer would be smelling the pine scent instead of a human odor—that deer have this amazing sense of smell, far better than that of human's. Who knew that, right?

The first two hours we were in the blind nothing at all happened, and Luke kept saying we couldn't talk at all, except in low whispers. But around 5:00 or so, this doe came into Elly's backyard, and all of a sudden this change came over Luke. He tensed up, eased his crossbow onto his knee, and stared intently at that deer. When it got to within about 20 yards of us, Luke raised the bow, clicked off something (later he called it a "safety") and shot. I saw the arrow hit the deer and it ran back toward the woods and had barely made it inside when it fell to the ground and didn't move. Luke pumped his fist and shouted, "Got her, meat for the winter."

We went out to the dead deer, and Luke said we would start "field dressing" her, which meant taking out all the inside organs I found out later. After a while, it seemed like Luke wasn't going to save those organs, and I asked if I could bring them home for my family to eat. I've seen Poppa butcher animals before and save the heart, tongue, liver, and kidneys for Mama to cook. I figured that Mama would be really happy for me to bring home some free food. He said sure, and he saved all those organs for me and cleaned them up, too. I don't think Elly's mom was too thrilled about me borrowing a cooler from her and putting the organs and ice in it, but she was nice about letting me do it anyway.

Not long after that, Luke's granddaddy picked him up, and Luke kissed me goodbye. And Elly and I went into her house for us to make a late dinner. It was really a great day.

Looking
at People
Differently

Chapter Twenty-Five: Luke

I didn't want to go play cornerback at football practice as my extra credit project for phys ed. But I also didn't want to do a stupid paper or Powerpoint or something for that project for Mr. Miley. I'm really trying to make better grades this year, partly because I want to, but also because Mia keeps telling me to. And I do want to make her happy and proud of me.

I'm up to 150 pounds and I'm now 5'9" and that's not going to cut it for the football team. I thought about backing out of going, but then Ms. Hawk heard about my going to practice and she said that would be a great idea for a sidebar or a short feature for Yearbook, a "What Football Practice Is Like" type piece she said and she assigned me to go do that and for Elly to go take pictures. Ms. Hawk said she would drive both Elly and me home after practice.

Once I realized I had to go to the practice for both Yearbook and Phys Ed 10, I decided that I didn't want to embarrass myself. The way Miley set things up (he's the defensive backs coach) was that I was going to try to cover Marcus one on one during passing practice drills—no contact, no tackling were the rules since I wouldn't be wearing pads. He said there was no way I would get hurt like that.

I told my best friend Allen about all that, and he said I had better call his brother Russell, who's been a football coach, and knows how things work. Russell told me that even though I had outrun Marcus in phys ed that I would have real trouble sticking with him on the field because Marcus had football instincts from all his years playing and I didn't. But what I had going for me, Russell said, was Caleb "and his scatter arm" and the likelihood that he and Marcus would want to humiliate me out on the field.

"They'll want to make you look bad the first two plays or so by throwing the deep ball," said Russell. "That'll flop because of Caleb's wild throws, Coach Dell will yell at him, and then send in a play for a slant or something like that. That's when you'll have a chance for an interception."

Sure enough, that's pretty much what happened. The first time Caleb passed, I followed Marcus deep and I was stride for stride with him and the ball sailed way over both our heads. The next time, Caleb tried to throw a deep ball with a little air under it, and I tipped the pass away from Marcus, and, boy, did Coach Dell yell at Caleb. On the third pass, I followed Marcus across the middle, keeping my eyes on his eyes the whole time like Russell had said to do. After Marcus made his cut, I looked around for the ball and intercepted it and started running.

The next thing I knew, somebody, it was that junior Jonathan I'm almost sure, hit me from behind and then that jerk Caleb hit me from the side, and I was down on the ground in absolute agony. Then somebody's cleats scraped across part of my back and left leg. My head was spinning and I looked down at my leg and my sweatpants were torn and there was blood everywhere. Yeah, so much for the no contact, nobody's getting hurt statement, right, Miley?

I rolled over and sat up and Marcus' brother Joshua was screaming at Caleb and Jonathan, "That was a cheap shot," and he cursed at both of them and Caleb and Jonathan hit him and then Marcus jumped into the middle of it and he hit Jonathan and everybody was yelling and screaming and cursing and Dell, Miley, and the other coaches were trying to break everybody up. I don't know what happened next. But I've got to say that I was surprised—and glad—that Marcus and his brother stood up for me. The next time I get a chance, I'm going to thank Marcus. I never would have thought he would have stood up for me like that.

Ms. Hawk and Elly came running over and helped me up, and Ms. Hawk said she would drive me to a doctor, and I told her that I would be fine. Granddaddy has said over and over his insurance is no good, and I knew we couldn't afford a trip to the doctor. Then Elly said to drop us off at her house, and she'd fix me up, so that's where we went.

When we got to Elly's house, nobody was at home, and I mean it was absolutely surreal. I'm lying face down on her living room sofa with a blanket under me, and my sweatshirt was off and my left pants leg was rolled up, and she was cleaning my wounds and spraying stuff and her parents walked in with her two brothers. Her dad let out a couple choice curse words and wanted to know what was going on and her mom ran into the hall and came back with more ointments and stuff. Finally the two of them finished bandaging me up and everybody except me went off into the kitchen.

I could hear loud voices going on in there, so I got up and decided I had better go apologize for being there. I didn't want Elly to get into trouble for being nice to me and I got to the door and heard Elly's dad say that, "We shouldn't have left that poor white trash along in our living room, he'll probably steal something."

I got really angry at that. I'm not trash. This year for the first time in my life, I've realized that I can be something. I know I'm not like my father. But I kept my temper under control. I've learned to do that from all those years when Dad would get into a rage against me. I knocked on the door and they said come in. And I said very politely, "Thank you for helping me, I'll be going home now."

I wanted to thank Elly, she was so nice to me. But if I had done that, it probably would just have made her dad madder at her. He offered to take me home, but I said I would walk. I didn't want to be in the same car with him. My leg hurt all the way home, but it was better than being in the same car with that man.

Chapter Twenty-Six: Elly

Lately, I've had to do some serious thinking about people that I thought I knew. When Ms. Hawk told Luke and me to go to football practice on Tuesday for a Yearbook story and photos, I had mixed emotions. I mean, I used to date Paul, I am dating Jonathan, I want to date Caleb, and the guy I have all these mixed up feelings for—Luke—and they were all going to be there. Talk about worlds colliding.

I don't know anything about football, but Luke sure didn't look like he should be out there practicing—all the guys were bigger than he was. I was trying to take pictures of him running after Marcus. Coach Dell had told him to cover Marcus. What's that mean anyway, cover with what? Anyway, they had been running around for a while and Luke caught this ball then Jonathan and Caleb came up behind Luke and knocked him down, and Caleb, it sure looked like he deliberately stepped on Luke's back and leg. I kept taking pictures, but then I stopped because Ms. Hawk was probably not going to want me to run photos of football players fighting each other. It was just crazy out there, Luke on the ground in pain, Marcus and his brother Joshua fighting Jonathan and Caleb. Why did Jonathan and Caleb do that to Luke—that can't be right? That's probably why Marcus and his brother got so mad.

When Ms. Hawk dropped Luke and me off at my house for me to patch up Luke, I got all these strange feelings when I was putting ointment and bandages on Luke. He kept apologizing to me for being there, and thanking me at the same time, and I was touching his back and his leg, and he was so sweet to me. And I had all these feelings for him, like I sometimes get.

I would never, ever flirt with Luke and try to steal him from Mia. She's really my best friend now, and I talk with her at lunch and after school more than anybody now. But, still... Luke, the more I'm around him and the way he's changed from being with Mia...

I didn't like it when Dad called Luke trash; he is not, maybe his dad is, but he's not. Dad is always talking about Caleb and what a great guy he is and how his family is so good, but Luke would never have snuck up from behind somebody and deliberately try to hurt them like Caleb and Jonathan did. I love my dad so much, but that was ugly the way he talked about Luke. Should I talk to Mom about the way Dad acted, should I ask her if she feels the same way about Luke? I can't believe that she does.

I wasn't happy with Jonathan, either, and the way he acted. The next day, I saw him during lunch and asked why he had come up behind Luke like that and hit him, and he told me that he was angry that Luke and me had come to practice together. I told him that was just stupid, that I was the photo editor for Yearbook and Ms. Hawk had told me to cover practice and she was there, too. "I wasn't 'with Luke,' I was doing what a teacher had told me to go do," was what I said.

Right then and there, I thought about breaking up with Jonathan, but I don't like to do things the spur of the moment, I like to think about things before going off and doing something I might regret later. Jonathan could see that I was angry when I said all that, and he started apologizing and said he would take me out to a nice restaurant Saturday night to make up. I said I would go, but I don't feel good about myself for saying that. Maybe it would be a mistake to keep dating Jonathan.

Maybe I should get over my stupid obsession with Caleb, too. But he is so good looking, and honest to goodness, I think he has been flirting with me lately. I've lost some more weight, and I only have five more pounds to go and Caleb several times has told me how good I look and that I have nice legs—he's really been turning on the charm. But he never noticed me when I was overweight; he hardly would even talk to me when I would try to flirt with him. And there's like this mean side to him that's very disturbing. The way he hit Luke and stomped on him from behind, the things he says in World History II class, I don't think I feel that way about things. I don't think Caleb likes the fact that Hispanics and Asians are at our school, except he didn't mind dating that Asian girl Amber that transferred here at the start of school. But she dumped him, I wonder why? Did she see the same things in him that I do now?

I've got to do some serious thinking. Maybe I need to look at people differently.

Chapter Twenty-Seven: Marcus

I never would have thought I would have gotten into a fight to protect Joshua, after all the ragging he has done on me. Joshua and I have had our issues since I started high school, but yesterday when Caleb and Jonathan took swings at him at football practice, I couldn't let that slide. I mean, he's my brother. I never thought Caleb and I would get into a fight, either, but that's just what happened.

I guess Caleb was mad that Luke had intercepted his pass. I get that, but Luke didn't make Caleb throw the ball wild. Caleb and Jonathan shouldn't have come up behind Luke and cheap shotted him. When Joshua shoved Caleb off Luke, he should never have hit my brother. Then Jonathan piled on Joshua, and I just snapped. The four of us were fighting and cussing, then the coaches and players were trying to break us up. It was just chaos—all because Coach Miley got this bright idea that Luke should try out for cornerback.

Actually, it wasn't such a bad idea. I mean, the kid has got some serious speed. After the fight was over, Joshua went over to Luke and thanked him for being there and asked him to consider trying out next year, that "We could use somebody with your speed." A couple days later before English class, I told Luke the same thing, that I was impressed with his speed. I had never even talked much, if at all, to Luke before. But he's an all right guy. He told me he really appreciated my sticking up for him at football practice when the fight was going on, but football just isn't his sport. I respect that, but we still could have used him next year.

It's no secret that this season is down the tubes. Because of the way Caleb and Jonathan acted at practice, Coach Dell suspended both of them for this Friday's game. We're 3 and 5 with two games left, and we're not going to any playoffs this year. That means fewer chances for college coaches to see me play. The playoffs are the best time to show your stuff for the recruiters because there are more of them around for those games than any other time. Of course, part of the reason we're not going to playoffs was my fault for being suspended the first two games. That's on me.

Really the only good thing to come out of the fight was how Joshua has been treating me ever since it happened. You know what he said when we were driving home from practice? "I've never been more proud of you. Thank you for sticking up for me. You're not a whiny kid anymore, you're becoming a man." Ever since the fight, he's been treating me more as an equal. When we got home that night, he even told Mom and Dad what happened and praised me in front of them. Dad said he did not approve of us fighting, but this one time it was justified. That it was right for Joshua to take up for Luke when he was lying on the ground, and that it was right for me to take up for my brother when he was cheap shotted. "You've always got to try to do the right thing in life," said Dad.

Mom chimed in and said she agreed with Dad, and she was proud of us both. So it was a real huggy-squeezy moment at our house the other night. It's never a bad thing when your parents are happy with you.

Except for the football season being the pits, life's not so bad this year. My grades are a lot better this year, I'm actually enjoying some of my classes, especially World History II. Mr. Wayne is a really good teacher, and the stuff we've been studying has been pretty interesting. The bubonic plague in

Europe, all those wars over religion, the settling of America…
that's pretty interesting stuff if you think about it. Before this
year, I never would have thought about it. I just would have
crammed the night before the test and then forgot everything I
had learned by the next day.

Maybe I should major in history in college. That would be
interesting. I mean I probably won't ever use the stuff anyway,
since I'm going to be a pro football player. But I have to major
in something, so it might as well be something that I'm
interested in. Of course, when I'm through playing professional
football, I won't need any money since I'll be set for life,
financially. So it's not like I would ever teach or do something
like that.

Oh, one more thing, Kylee told me she was proud of me
too about the fight thing. She said she has seen a big change in
me this year and likes what she sees. She said she was proud to
be my girlfriend and was really glad that we had gotten back
together. So in spite of all the crap that went on this week, all
things considered I had a pretty good week. When you've got
your parents, your brother, and your girlfriend praising you,
you're doing all right.

Chapter Twenty-Eight: Mia

I have to say that Elly is my best friend among all my girlfriends, but I still don't understand some things about her. Like when I spent that recent Saturday night at her house. She is so obsessed over her appearance and clothes and makeup and stuff like that—it's almost as if she is neurotic about it. When I got there, she said she wanted to show me some new outfits her mom had bought for her since she had been on a diet. I can tell that she has lost weight, and I told her that and that she looks pretty. But I also said that I thought she looked pretty when she was heavier, and I meant that sincerely.

"That's not what boys think about chubby girls," she said.

"Who cares what immature boys think," I told her. I then told her that white guys, black guys, Hispanic guys, Asian guys—they all need to grow up, well at least the vast majority of them do from what I've seen. I'm not going to spend my high school years trying to fit into some stereotype of what my figure is supposed to be like, what kind of makeup I'm supposed to wear, and what kind of clothes I have to wear. I just don't care. I'm happy with myself.

Then Elly said she agreed with all that, but then she said, "Still...," which really meant that though she agreed with what I said, she wasn't going to change her outlook. Then she got out some new blush and eye shadow that she had bought for her dates with Jonathan and asked if I wanted to try them on and I started to say, "Not really." But then I thought that would hurt her feelings, so I said okay. I admit that it was fun to put that stuff on and seeing how I looked with a lot of makeup was interesting, but that wasn't the real me with all that stuff on my face. I've worn a little makeup when I've been out with Luke. I've worn my newest jeans a couple times. We've talked about going out to dinner at a nice restaurant when he can drive on his own, and I want to wear my Sunday dress when we go do that, and maybe put my hair up some kind of way or sweep it around so that it falls over one of my shoulders. I would definitely wear some makeup when we go out to dinner that time, but not a whole lot. We talked about the expense of going out to dinner, but then we both agreed that we could go do some extra job and dedicate that money to us going out to eat somewhere nice. Neither one of has ever been out to what Poppa calls "a sit-down restaurant," and I'd like to experience that.

Elly finally got off the weight and makeup topic, and then she wanted to show me some of her new skirts and dresses that she and her mom have bought shopping since Elly has lost weight. Some of the dresses were exactly the same, except maybe they were a little shorter or a size smaller from the ones she already had. It just seemed like such a waste of money. I didn't tell her that, though.

The next topic was guys, and she said she wasn't real happy dating Jonathan and asked what I thought about him, and I told her the truth… that I had only ever had him in one class ever and I didn't have any feelings one way or the other about him. He just seemed like a typical guy, which was sort of an insult, and I thought Elly took it that way, too. Then she said that Caleb had been flirting with her a lot lately and that he was her dream guy and what did I think of her maybe breaking up with Jonathan and really letting Caleb know she was available?

I don't like Caleb. I do know him, and I think he is cruel and immature and has a totally undeserved high opinion of himself. Yeah, he is super good looking, but so what. He doesn't have a kind heart. He just goes from girl to girl because he thinks life is like that. What a jerk. But I didn't think I could tell Elly that.

She kept pestering and pestering me about Caleb and finally I said, "You can do better than Caleb, Elly, a lot better. It would be a mistake to go out with him." That was about the nicest thing I could say about Caleb. I could tell my comments upset her a little, and I hadn't wanted that to happen, but she shouldn't have insisted so much about me giving some sort of opinion about him. Elly should be glad that I didn't tell her what I really thought.

Then Elly wanted to know what it was like to be dating Luke, and I said it was "Absolutely wonderful, that it was as good as I thought it would be." That he was kind and attentive to me and cared about my thoughts and opinions on things and that he treated me with respect. Maybe, I shouldn't have gone on and on like that. Maybe, it sounded like I was bragging about having such a great boyfriend. I don't want to ever come off like that. But Luke is great. Elly said I should hang on to Luke, and I smiled and said, "I intend to."

I was really upset when a few days later, Elly called me and said that Luke had been injured at football practice when Caleb and Jonathan came up from behind and tackled or hit him or something. Luke is too small to be playing football, even for extra credit or whatever the reason he was out there, and I had told him that. But he said Coach Dell had told him that there would be no tackling or physical contact. I asked Elly about that, and she said Caleb and Jonathan had broken the rules and got suspended from the football team for a game because of what they did to Luke. That should tell her all she needs to know about the two "boys" in her life. Elly is a wonderful, kind person, but she's making bad choices about guys.

Good Classes/ Bad Classes

Chapter Twenty-Nine: Luke

Things finally hit rock bottom in Geometry class right before Christmas break. We were reviewing for our big test at the end of the semester and poor Ms. Waters was trying to get people to listen to her. But as usual only about four or five of the kids in the room were, and one of those was me, and I didn't know what the heck she was lecturing about. She was explaining how to measure angles and something about the angle of elevation of a triangle, which had just followed the lesson on theorems and proofs—real head exploding crap that nobody will ever use in life unless they become a geometry teacher. I looked around the room and some of the kids were on Twitter, some were on Instagram and showing each other pictures, a couple more were asleep, and the rest were texting or listening to music.

And the woman just snapped. She walked over to Thomas, who never pays any attention to her and said, "Hand over your phone and give me your earbuds, too." School policy says that students can only listen to music if teachers give them permission to do so after work is done for the day. The policy also says that student use of phones is at the discretion of the teacher, which basically means that a kid can't have his phone out unless the student is using it for research or to take notes or if the student has been given permission. Thomas just ignored Ms. Waters, and she said, "One more time, give me your phone," and again he ignored her, and she just snatched it out of his hands and began walking away.

Well, this caused Thomas to cuss at her, and the next thing I knew he and three of his fellow losers were yelling at Ms. Waters. He was threatening and following her up to her desk and kept on cursing at her the whole time. Some of the students started taking videos of what was going on to post online, like it was all some kind of big joke. The weird thing was that for about the first time all year, everybody was focused on Ms. Waters. I never act up in there. I can't stand a lot of the people in that room. I understand their frustration, but they have like this open hostility toward her. That's just wrong. Ms. Waters is a first year-teacher, and I guarantee you that none of the classes she took in college prepared her for us. I don't know what's going on in Geometry anymore than anybody else, but some of the kids are just plain cruel to that woman.

So Thomas was cursing at Ms. Waters and was threatening to hit her if she didn't give back his phone, and she just started to bawl. I felt so bad for her that I got out of my chair, went over to the intercom and hit the emergency button and said we needed an administrator in the room immediately. Ms. Waters and Thomas both looked at me and she said thank you. Then Thomas sent some choice profanity my way and said he and his boys were going to take care of me right now before Mr. Caldwell or whoever arrived.

I moved in between Thomas and Ms. Waters, because I was afraid that he was going to do something to her and I told him, "Yeah, only a tough dude like you would hit a woman. If you touch her, I'll beat the crap out of you!"

Thomas came firing up to me and got in my face and about that second, Mr. Caldwell rushed into the room and yelled at me and Thomas to follow him to his office. I was shaking. I don't know if it was from anger or fear… maybe both. I might have gotten in a few shots at Thomas, but sooner or later he and his buddies would've beaten me to a pulp. Caldwell then looked over at Ms. Waters and saw her crying, then he used his walky-talky to ask the school resource officer to come watch the class. He also told Ms. Waters to come to his office, too, when the resource officer arrived. I've been bullied before, especially when I was in middle school and a ninth grader, and I wasn't going to stand by and let that jerk Thomas bully Ms. Waters.

The four of us got to Mr. Caldwell's office, and Ms. Waters blurted out, bless her, that I was the one who had used the intercom to call him and that I had gotten out of my chair to protect her, that Thomas had threated physical violence against her. Caldwell, then said, "Thomas, what have you got to say for yourself?"

He said, "She took my phone without asking me," which is about the dumbest thing he could have said.

"Did you threaten her with physical violence?" Caldwell then asked and Thomas cursed at him and said yeah and then it was Caldwell's turn to come flying out of his desk.

"You're suspended for 10 days," said Caldwell. "You can come back to school on the 11th day providing one of your parents is present to hear what the consequences will be the next time this type of behavior is shown."

After that, Thomas was sent to where the secretary sits so he could wait for somebody to pick him up, Ms. Waters went back to her room, and it was just Caldwell and me in his office.

"Thank you for standing up for Ms. Waters, Luke, I really appreciate that," he said.

"I appreciate you saying that, but you know Thomas is not going to let this rest until he gets even with me," I said. "Sooner or later, he and his pals are going to jump me in there. I'm begging you. You've got to help Ms. Waters control that class."

"I'll see what I can do," said Caldwell. He started looking at the master schedule and then it looked like he went under the administrator part of Power School, and I heard him mutter under his breath, "Every student in there has a *D* or *F* average."

Which was a surprise to me because I thought everyone was failing. He did some more scanning around and then he told me that Thomas and all three of his buddies were getting schedule changes for the second semester, that none of them would be in Ms. Waters room and none of them would be in the same math class together.

So I guess the high point of Geometry class for me for the year will be that I won't get beaten up in there, that my other great accomplishment for the year will be that I will hopefully have a high to medium *F*...whoopee-do.

Chapter Thirty: Elly

I love ending the school day with Yearbook seventh period. There's pressure to meet deadlines, but Ms. Hawk has got everything so organized, and everybody in there wants to be in that class and create something that people will want to have for the rest of their lives, and it's just fun and meaningful to be a part of something like that.

I really like being on Luke and Mia's team, too. Sitting around with them and planning what we're going to cover on our spreads. And see what kind of pictures I will need to take and how we will lay out the copy and photos so that a spread is visually appealing. There's time for us to talk about school and things while we're working on some project, and that's nice, too.

The other day, we started talking about what we were going to do over the Christmas holidays, and I started telling about how Dad was going to take everybody to the beach for four days because he had found a condo really cheap to rent and it would be nice to get away and eat at some really great fresh seafood places and go to some museums down there. Then I realized that saying something like that might have been hurtful to Mia and Luke because they wouldn't have any concept what it would be like to have money to spend on "getting away from it all," and I was ashamed of what I had said… maybe I had sounded braggy.

So I quickly decided to change the subject and asked them what they were going to do for the holidays. I meant what they were going to do as individuals, but both of them started telling me what they were going to do together. Mia said the thing they were going to do that she was looking forward to the most was going on an all-day six-mile hike in the national forest for their Ecology project. That Luke had come up with the idea to ask Ms. Jenkins if they could research what birds they found and whether they were year-round residents, winter residents, or just passing through because of present weather conditions. Then he and Mia would also make note of what kind of habitats they found the birds in and what were the likely foods the birds were feeding on in those micro-habitats and that would be their research project for Ecology.

Mia said she was in charge of lunch and snacks and that Luke said he would identify and find sassafras roots and they would steep them over a campfire and have that to drink while they were cooking their lunch. Right after they had told me about that, Ms. Hawk asked Luke to come talk to her about something on one of his spreads, and I asked Mia if her parents were okay with her going off deep in the woods with Luke. I said I knew Luke would never do anything wrong, but were her parents understanding about them being alone like that?

Mia said that her mom had told her earlier that month that she had tried and tried not to like Luke, and her mom had hoped by not trying to talk her out of dating him, that eventually Mia would see that she could do better. But then her mom said, "The more I'm around Luke, the more I like him. Honestly, I don't see how you could find someone better."

I said I was surprised to hear that and asked her if her dad felt the same way and Mia confessed that she and her mom still had not told him about Luke and her being together, that he still thought that the only thing the two of them had in common was their L&M Enterprises business. We then started talking about Christmas and getting presents for our family, and I said I didn't know what to get Jonathan, that I was dreading buying him something, that what I really wanted to do was break up with him before Christmas because it was just a waste of time to keep dating him.

Then Mia said, "I don't understand why you would go out with somebody you don't like, it doesn't make sense." Which really made me think. Then she said she and Luke had decided what to get each other for Christmas, that they had talked about it and talked about it and finally they decided that she would make him a sweater and he would buy her a baby goat. I laughed out loud at the goat thing, but then I realized she was serious.

Luke and her had come up with the idea of raising five goats in his granddaddy's yard. They had ordered five young goats and one of them was for her, and they would raise the goats until they got bigger, then sell them as an organic health food. They would also make a bunch of money off their goats, just like they had made off the chickens when Luke helped her expand the chicken run.

About that time, Luke came back, and I said, "Mia told me about the goats, you two can make money off just about anything."

Mia next said, "Tell her about that $150 you made off your writing." Luke said Ms. Hawk had encouraged him to try to publish the article he had written for English, "The Day Granddaddy and I Went Deer Hunting," and Luke said that he had sent the story to Lindsay Thomas, the editor of *Quality Whitetails*, which is Luke's favorite deer hunting magazine. That Mr. Thomas had bought the article for the Fire Pot section of the magazine and asked Luke to send some more stories in for consideration. Luke said he was going to try to write some fishing stories for magazines, too... that maybe he could write more and stop having to work so hard on the lawn mowing business, that he and Mia could start maybe getting more into the goat, chicken, and livestock end, maybe they could raise a beef cow next and there would be more money in that than lawn care.

When I listened to all that, I realized that Luke and Mia would never be jealous of me going off to the beach, that they were the lucky ones because they were going to be together during Christmas and loving being together. When I got home that afternoon, I called Jonathan and broke up with him. I feel good about my decision.

Chapter Thirty-One: Marcus

Before the year started, I was absolutely sure about how a bunch of things would turn out and almost nothing happened like I thought it would. Take the football season, for instance. We ended up 4 and 6, I missed four games because of the suspension and later a concussion, and Caleb and I never got on the same page on the field and now we're barely even talking to each other at school. There were no playoffs, no first team district for me or anybody else, no college scouts at our last couple of games, and no team unity.

I thought Caleb and I would be hanging out and double dating, but that all fell apart, too. I used to think it was cool for him to be juggling two or three girls at a time, but now he just seems pathetic in the way he looks at girls as something to conquer. I know I shouldn't talk too much because I was basically doing the same thing last year. But now I realize it's best just to have a steady girlfriend, like Kylee... a girl that will get all over me when I mess up, but will let me know when she's proud of me, too. The other day she told me how proud she was of my school grades, that they were more important in the long run than my accomplishments on the football field. I don't know if that is really true or not, but it's a whole lot better for her and my parents and Joshua praising me for my improved grades and attitude than being all over my case, like they were last year.

I'm actually liking some of my classes this year, especially history. Everything Mr. Wayne has gone over this semester has been really interesting. The Black Death wiping out a whole lot of Europe, all those wars of religion and the Catholics and Protestants slaughtering each other, the American Revolution and the Founding Fathers and how many of them knew slavery was wrong but didn't know how to deal with it… the French Revolution, Robespierre and all those people going to the guillotine. The other night, Kylee and I went out to dinner and somehow we got on the topic of history and we must have talked about history stuff for most of our meal.

She told me that I maybe should major in history in college, that she could see me really getting into it and maybe even teaching history in high school or college. I've never really thought about what I would do after college besides playing professional sports. But she told me I should have a backup plan and after the way things went this football season, I had better have an alternative. I asked Joshua about my majoring in history and he told me that was a smart idea, that I would probably do really well with that.

Joshua has been treating me more as an equal. A couple of times this month late at night after my homework was done, I've knocked on his door and asked to come in and talk about things that were on my mind. He told me that Jordan really thinks I've grown up and she enjoys being around me now when Kylee and I double date with them. I never thought Jordan would say anything nice about me. Joshua and Jordan have been dating for way over two years now, and I asked him what was the secret of their relationship, and he said respect and compromise. That they treat each other with respect and if the two of them can't decide on something or another, each one gives in a little bit on a particular issue, then both of them feel that they got something out of the agreement. That makes sense and I told Kylee what Joshua had said about having respect for someone and being willing to compromise, and she said it made all the sense in the world.

I'm back on the basketball team and this year I've been starting both in practice and our early non-conference games. The only good thing about football season ending so early was that I got to rejoin the basketball team much earlier than last year. Our point guard Quintin and I have been on the same page from the get-go. He's just a junior, but he's got senior-type leadership skills. Joshua recognized that trait in him, too, and told me to develop trust in him and to tell him that I trusted him to get me the ball in the best possible position for me to do something with it.

The other night we were playing King which has a pretty good team, and we were at their place. We got off to a slow start and were down by five in the second half, but Quintin and I got out on a 2 on 1 fast break and their power forward was tight on me as I drove to the basket. Last year, I would have tried to have out-quicked my way past him, but this time I faked like I was going up for a layout but at the last second I dumped it off to Quintin for an easy deuce.

The next time down we were on defense, Quintin intercepted a pass and we had another 2 on 1 with only the King shooting guard trying to stop us. Quinten did like this super ball fake to me, then turned on the speed like he was going to take it himself to the rack, then at the last second threw an alley-oop to me for a big-time jam. After King scored, we went on a 9-0 run and by the start of the fourth quarter, we were up 12 and for all intents and purposes, the game was over. Later, Coach Henson told me my pass to Quintin changed the whole game, and Joshua told me the same thing on the way home when he and Dad were dissecting the game. Maybe basketball will be my best shot at the pros, maybe majoring in history would work out great for me, too.

Chapter Thirty-Two: Mia

For my World History II research project first semester, I read this great book, *1491*, that Mr. Wade recommended to me. It's all about what the Americas were like before Columbus came in 1492. I was amazed to learn that the Aztecs had a civilization that was in many ways superior to what was in Europe because they had running water, great cities, and a larger population. That got me to thinking about how destructive the Europeans and especially the Spanish were when they came to what is today Mexico—how they left my grandparents and ancestors' country much poorer and worse off.

Mama has told me that my family has both Spanish and Native American heritage, and she thinks a little Caucasian, too. And all this got me to thinking, too, about maybe one day returning to Texas, where my grandparents lived for a time when they came to this country illegally, or maybe even Mexico because we still have family there, too. Maybe, I could become a doctor and help poor people get medical care—that maybe I could do something to make life a little better for people that are struggling. I could open a general practice or perhaps be a pediatrician if I just wanted to concentrate on helping children.

I asked Mama again about what did she think about me doing something like that, and she said that would be fantastic, that she could see me being really fulfilled as a person if I spent my life helping people as a doctor. I know she's worried that I won't get enough scholarship money to do this. At night, Luke and I talk all the time over the phone about school, our business, and what we want to do with our lives, and I just had to ask him what he thought about me going to Mexico or Texas and being a doctor. And he said that would be great, that he could see me doing something like that and being "super at it."

I wanted to ask him if we were still together then would he go with me, but I just couldn't… that would be too forward. I confess, sometimes I think what it would be like to be married to him. I know that's silly with us only being sophomores. But don't all girls think about what it would be like to marry the boy they are dating at the time, even girls who are sophomores in high school? I bet a lot of them do. I can't imagine ever wanting to break up with Luke. He's the type of boy I always dreamed I would want to date.

One of the reasons I've been thinking about that was the subject came up when we were reading *Lord of the Flies* in Ms. Hawk's English 10 Honors class. She asked whether high school boys or girls would do better if they were stranded on a deserted island like the one the small boys in the novel were stranded on. Somehow or the other when the girls were arguing that we would do better while the boys were arguing with us that they would do better, Ms. Hawk asked what did the two sexes look for in a leader or in a spouse. And she asked if any of us ever thought about those things. Of course, none of the guys who volunteered their thoughts had thought anything about the type of girl who would make a good leader or wife, but a lot of the girls said they had thought about it. Camila, Hannah, and Jasmine said they thought all the time about the type of guy that they wanted to marry, and Kylee said high school was a time to sort of "try on guys for size to see what we liked." Then Caleb said something sarcastic like, "Guys aren't a pair of shoes to be thrown away." That's not what Kylee meant and he knew that.

Then all of a sudden, Mary asked me whether I ever thought about marrying Luke, and I got so red in the face, but I was mad, too, that she asked that in front of everybody. I looked over at Luke, we always sit next to each other in all the classes we're in together, and he looked at me and didn't say anything. I said that question was "personal," and I didn't want to talk about it. Later in the day when we were in the library reading and talking together, Luke told me not to worry about what Mary said, that I made him happy, and he was grateful and thankful for me being in his life, and we would see what the future brought for us. It was a sweet thing for him to say, and it was just one more reason, I'm lucky to spend time with him.

Later on that week in Ms. Hawk's class right before Christmas break, we finished reading *Lord of the Flies*. Mrs. Hawk said for our culminating activity we were going to play what she called the Island Game. It's a game she created where all the students in her class are stranded on the same island that the boys in *Lord of the Flies* crash landed on. The assignment was for the class members to try to create a society, and the question was would we be able to stay together as a group or would we fracture into cliques. We would also have to pick a leader for the whole group or if we broke into cliques, we would pick a leader for each individual group.

I thought we could stay together and work together, but things fell apart almost immediately. Most of the boys wanted Caleb as the guy leader and Leigh as the female leader, but when we girls voted for leader, Allen and Luke tied for the male role, and the girls voted for me as the female leader. I couldn't believe that the guys wanted Caleb to lead, what does being a first class jerk have to do with leading people in a crisis situation. I like Leigh all right, but as I heard Mary whisper to Paige, the guys wanted Leigh to lead so that they could gawk at her legs when she was giving instructions for the day.

Finally, all of the girls except Leigh and Amber (they went with the guys—good luck with that decision) decided to form a group, and we asked Luke and Allen to come with us and they could hunt and fish for food, and we would build the shelters and cook. I know those are stereotypical roles, but none of us know anything about hunting and fishing and Luke and Allen sure do. I think we would do just fine as a group and that's what I wrote in the journal that Ms. Hawk assigned. I am so glad to be with Luke.

Changes

Chapter Thirty-Three: Luke

After Christmas, the first thing I noticed in Ms. Waters' Geometry class was that it looked a lot smaller. Of course, I had already known that Thomas and his boys were gone to other math classes, but it just seemed smaller somehow. Ms. Waters looked stern when we were coming into the room, and the first thing she said was that she was passing around two plastic tubs, one for us to put our music devices in and the other to put our cell phones in. Of course, I can't afford to have either, but that's just the way it is. It would be nice to have a phone where I could look up things online and text Mia and Allen and also see what the current weather was when I was getting ready to go fishing or hunting or hiking. But it's not the end of the world that I don't have one.

Some of the guys and girls started arguing with Ms. Waters about the new rules and she snapped and said, "It's not open to discussion. Put them in the tubs or you can tell your sorrows to Mr. Caldwell." People could tell she wasn't bluffing. Lots of times the first semester, she would say that such and such was going to be the way it was going to be from now on, or there was going to be a new rule, but she never followed through, so the kids started ignoring her. But this time when she was fussing at us, her voice had an edge—a sharpness—to it, and then she gave the people who complained a long, hard stare after she snapped at them, so pretty soon the only sounds in the room were that of electronic devices being dropped into plastic boxes.

Not long after that, Mr. Caldwell came into the room and said, "How are things going today, Ms. Waters," and his voice had an edge to it, too. I don't know if Caldwell told her to crack down on us or she did it on her own and his visit was just a coincidence. I don't care either. I just want some order in that room, so Ms. Waters can give me some individual help and I can make a low *D* for the year and get out of Geometry. Spending my junior year repeating this awful class would be the absolute worst.

Mia has insisted that we spend lunch together every Monday through Thursday going over my Geometry work for the day and her drilling me on this crap. She said our Friday book clubs during lunch would continue as always. I would be happy doing anything with her—well maybe not math—but I'm desperate to pass, so I agreed to do what she said. When I took my Thursday Geometry quiz, I got a high *D* on it, the first time all year I've passed a quiz. It did seem easier than the other quizzes that I've taken and failed. Was it because of all of Mia's tutoring or was it because Ms. Waters has dumbed down the class because just about all of us are failing? Or maybe she has made it easier because Mr. Caldwell told her to dumb it down because of all the failures. I don't care what the answer for that is, either. I am now the proud owner of a *D* average in Geometry after the first week of the second semester. I think this is what they call one of "life's little victories."

When I got home from school on Thursday, Granddaddy told me he wanted to have a long talk with me. I could tell he was upset or something when I came home. Granddaddy said he wasn't going to beat around the bush and asked if I had known that Dad had been drinking heavily since Mom died. I said I hadn't known, but I just had assumed that that had been the case. Then there was this long pause, and granddaddy said, "Your father was in a car wreck last night when he was on his way to work. He passed away this afternoon. I didn't know whether to tell you or not before school that he had been in a wreck. I'm sorry."

Granddaddy went on to say what Dad's blood alcohol content was, but I wasn't really listening. The first thought that came into my mind was whether anybody else had been involved in the accident. It would have been awful if dad had killed somebody else when he was swerving around on the road. But, no, Granddaddy said it had been a one-car accident, which was good, we both agreed.

I didn't feel anything when I heard about Dad. I wasn't sorry, I wasn't happy, I wasn't relieved that he apparently hadn't suffered much because Granddaddy said that Dad had never regained consciousness. I was just glad that he hadn't killed somebody besides himself. Does that make me a bad person because those were the types of thoughts that went through my head? I hope not, I don't know for sure, though. I hadn't seen or heard from Dad, not even for Christmas, since I ran away from home. So now for sure I'll never see him again. I don't feel bad or good about that, either. I don't know what I feel...

After Granddaddy and I got through talking, I called Mia and told her about Dad, and her only concern, like always, was how was I, was I okay, would I be all right, should she come over? I said I was fine, and she didn't need to come over. Like what would she have told her father, the man who thinks I'm the "boy who works for Mia;" that she was going to visit the hired help who had lost a family member? No, that wouldn't have been good for her to try to explain that visit. But I felt so much better after we talked about 10 minutes. I don't even remember what we talked about. She was there for me and that was more than enough.

Chapter Thirty-Four: Elly

When my family was at the beach over the Christmas Holidays, I got this text from Mary saying the word was that Caleb and his girlfriend had broken up and "now's your chance." When it comes to rumors and who's dating or talking with someone, Mary is never wrong so my imagination just went wild. For the first time in my life, I really like the way I look. I've lost all that weight I needed to lose, my hair is much longer, my contacts are working out just great, and I've been getting a lot of compliments from Paige, Mary, and Camila and just about everybody else about how good I look. Yeah, I can make a play for Caleb.

I texted Mary back asking if she thought I should text Caleb and if I did, what should I text him about. And would it be too obvious or maybe make me seem aggressive or desperate if I did text him... what should I do? Mary texted right back asking if I had any photos of me in a bikini at the beach and that if so, I could post them on Instagram and then send out a text to all my friends about what a great time my family and I were having at the beach and write about the photos being on Instagram. That way it wouldn't be obvious that I was just trying to get Caleb to notice how great I look now. The only problem with that was that it had been raining there except for one day and that day when I did try to get in the water a little while wearing my new bikini, I got chill bumps so bad that I had to go back to our rental house almost immediately. So that idea was no good.

Then Mary texted back and said to text Caleb about needing some help in some class and asking for advice and then see where that got me. But I texted back that I would never ask Caleb for help in any class, nobody would. And Mary sent back a text in all caps saying, "THAT'S NOT THE POINT, IDIOT. ACT LIKE YOU NEED HELP FROM HIM."

I just couldn't wrap my head around asking Caleb for help with school work, so finally I decided to wait until I got back to school the first week in January. I convinced Mom that I needed a new mini-skirt, so we went shopping while we were at the beach. I figured I could wear that skirt the first day back to show Caleb how great I look now.

But when we were driving back home, I got a text from Mary saying that she just got word that Caleb was going with somebody new, and my mind just went crazy on who it could have been in our sophomore class or maybe Caleb had found some freshman girl; those ninth grade females would just go nuts to be with him. Instead, Mary texted back that Rachel, "You know, that junior girl in Spanish II class," was Caleb's "new conquest."

I couldn't believe it. It's bad enough having competition from the sophomore girls in our class and all those goofy ninth grade girls, but having to worry about junior females, too…it's just unfair. I was so upset that I texted Mary that I didn't want to talk about it anymore. When we got home the night before the second semester started, I called Mary for her to give me the latest, and I told her flat out, I couldn't believe that Caleb was dating a junior. But Mary said, "It makes all the sense in the world," and all I could think to ask was "How so."

Then Mary said, "Because Caleb can now go to the prom because Rachel is a junior, and Rachel can have one of the hottest guys in the school on her arm. It's a win-win for both of them." Mary was right, of course, that scenario makes all the sense in the world. Then she said, "Look, you won't be single long. The word is out about you and Jonathan breaking up, too. Give it a week and some guy will start talking to you and trying to figure out if you're interested in that primitive male way they have of doing things."

Mary was right. In lunch on Wednesday, Matthew from Spanish II class dropped by our lunch table and asked if I had time to help him with the vocabulary words, so I did. Then he dropped by on Thursday and asked for help on a verb lesson, and this time I wasn't shocked that he had come by, so I had had time to think about whether I would mind going out with him, and I decided he would be okay. I mean, he's fairly good looking and I know he's on the basketball team and I think his position is forward or something, you know, the position where they stand under the basket a lot and wait for something to happen, then shove and push each other around trying to pick up the ball or put it in the basket or keep it from going in the basket or goal or something stupid like that. The good thing about basketball games is that they're not outside in the cold like football games, and the bleachers are warmer to sit on than those cold, metal seats next to the football field are. I'm through dating football players.

Anyway on Friday, Matthew came up to me during lunch and said he knew that it was short notice, but would I like to go out for pizza after the home game on Friday night, and I said that would be great with all the enthusiasm I could summon up. I mean, I think he will be okay to go out with. It's better than sitting home and listening to my brothers argue about some ridiculous video game and who has the better all-time score.

Chapter Thirty-Five: Marcus

Friday night before the game, we were doing just normal pre-game lay-up drills when all of a sudden Quintin pulled up lame. It was a tight hamstring or something. He's one of the best point guards in the whole region and a real team leader as a junior. We really don't have anybody that could replace him because the backup point guard is a freshman and he's just not ready to play at this level yet. After Quintin went down, Coach Henson came over to me and said that he needed me to do something really important for the team. "After Quintin, you're our best ball handler," he said. "Can you run the point just for tonight?"

I said I could and then while everybody else was warming up, Coach Henson put all this heavy duty stuff on me and kept saying that he knew I could handle it and run our set plays just fine. He said he wanted me to think pass first, but that the whole offense was to run through me, and I was not to shy away from shooting especially after I had established a solid passing game plan the first half—that I would be working mostly to set up other players the first half. Then the second half, I would likely get a lot of scoring opportunities because the other team would be playing me to pass more than to shoot. I really was excited about the extra challenge and responsibility and proud that Coach Henson trusted me to run the team.

The first half, it didn't take long for the team and me to get on the same page. Westside's center didn't have good quickness or speed, so I told our center Eric to sprint down the court on every change of possession, and I would feed him. We got three easy buckets in the first eight minutes just on that matchup advantage alone. Then I noticed that Matthew, our small forward, had a slight height and jumping advantage over Westside's forward, so I ran some plays to get Matthew the ball in the lane and he put in two floaters and an easy jumper from the foul line early on. Rasheed, our big forward, didn't have any matchup advantages versus their four guy, but the Westside starter picked up two quick fouls early on helping out on defending Eric, so I figured that he would sluff off some on Rasheed. That guess on my part proved true when Rasheed bulled by the guy on two straight possessions.

At the end of the first half, we were up 10, and I think I had only shot two or three times and made just one of them, but I was having so much fun distributing the ball that I hadn't even noticed that I wasn't getting many points. When we came into the locker room at half, Coach Henson just raved about my leadership and unselfishness to the rest of the team, and Quintin pounded me on the back and said I was doing an awesome job. I tell you I've never felt so good about my play on the court. Quintin even teased me that he was going to have trouble getting his point position back, and maybe he should be the shooting guard from now on.

Before we went back out for the second half, Coach Henson told me that the Westside point would likely be playing off me to start the half, and I was to take advantage of that. On the first possession, he told me to run a play where I sent the ball down deep to Eric and then have Eric immediately kick it back to me at the top of the key for a three. Then on the next possession, feed Matthew then have Eric set a screen for me, and then get the ball back from Matthew and for me to either take a short jumper behind Eric or drive to the hoop. "Let's blitz them early and put them away," said Henson.

And that's just what happened. I hit a nothing but net three on our first possession and on the second after Eric set the screen, I drove to the hoop and slammed it. We were up 15 and then Westside just fell apart. Mid-way through the fourth quarter, we were up 25 and Coach Henson put the subs in. My final stat line was 12 assists, 13 points, 10 rebounds, and 3 steals. I had never had a triple-double before; heck, I don't think I've ever had more than four rebounds in a game before. When I met Joshua and Jordan after the game, they were both raving about my play and Kylee said she was "proud of the way you played." Man, did I feel good.

We went out for pizza after the game, and a bunch of the guys and their girlfriends sat at the same table. We talked about the game for a little while, but then Kylee started talking about school and the neat stuff we were doing in World History II class, and Elly joined in about her project on Martin Luther, and I started talking about my research paper on the Renaissance. Elly looks really hot, I can see why Matthew asked her out.

Anyway, it was the first time I've ever really talked about school stuff when out with a group of people. It was kind of neat. I guess I have changed since last year. I guess I was "full of crap," a lot of the time as Joshua used to say. I've gone from hating history to thinking about majoring in it. It's never a bad night when your brother, your coach, and your girlfriend think you're awesome.

Chapter Thirty-Six: Mia

When Luke called me on Thursday night, I could tell something was wrong from the tone of his voice. He stuttered around for a while then blurted out that his dad had died from being in a car wreck. I didn't know what to say at first but then I realized that the most important thing to ask was if he was okay. Luke said he was fine but that he was wondering if I would mind going for a long hike in the national forest on Saturday for our weekly date. I said, "I would love to go anywhere with you, just to be with you would make me happy." I know that sounded forward, but I don't care. Luke needed me to help him sort through things, and the big changes that will happen because of his father's death. I wanted to be there for him.

Like always, we met a couple of miles from the national forest entrance and rode our bikes there and started hiking around 9. Almost immediately, Luke started talking non-stop about his dad's death and what that meant. Luke said that after his mom had died, his granddaddy and father had gone over the will, so his granddaddy knew exactly what the financial situation was.

Luke said that his granddaddy said that after his dad's debts were paid off and the house sold, there would likely be enough money for him to go to college for at least two years at some state school. Then he could use the money that he had earned from L&M Enterprises and his savings account to help finish the last two years of college without going into so much debt that it would take many, many years to pay off his loan. Luke asked me what I thought about all that and I just had to exclaim, "That's awesome, go for it!"

Luke smiled when I said that, but he said that wasn't even the best part. He said that his granddaddy had been saving money in a special account for Luke to go to college, and he also had other money from his regular savings account and that, anyway with there being no need to use that money for college now, they could use that money for something else. What was that I asked?

"Granddaddy wants for him and me to go looking for land to buy out in the country, so that I can have that place to go live on one day," said Luke. "That if we could buy the land and have it free and clear, I wouldn't have to borrow so much from the bank when it came time to build a house when I was older."

"That's wonderful, Luke," I blurted out. I could see how happy he was about the country land, and he gave me this big smile when I said how wonderful it was and then he stopped walking and held me in his arms and gave me the biggest hug and longest kiss that he's ever given me. I felt so close to him. My mind just started running wild and thinking what it would be like to be married to Luke and living out in the country and having enough space to raise chickens and goats and who knows what else. But then I thought about my dream to go to Texas or Mexico and become a doctor, and I didn't know which I would decide to do if I ever had to make a choice to stay here with Luke or go far away and practice medicine.

I mean, we're only sophomores and neither one of us has ever said, "I love you," because I think we both know that we're too young to really, truly know what love is. I just can't stand how some girls in our class talk about "loving" some boy and then two weeks later, they've broken up with that guy and are dating somebody else and now they "love" the new guy. That's not what love is. I know I don't know what true love is yet, but

I do think I know what love isn't… and I think Luke feels the same way about all that.

I spent so long thinking about all that, that Luke thought something was wrong and asked if I were okay, and I just decided right then and there to tell him exactly what I had been thinking about—what love is and how the students at school always are "in love" and what our future might be. Right then, Luke said, "Let's sit down against a tree and just talk." So we did. It was so good to know that he thought the same way I did about true love and how we were too young to really know about something like that.

"But I want to tell you this," he said. "You have made my life way better than it was. I am very, very thankful for you. Maybe one day when we're older, maybe one day we'll find that we love one another. Right now, you're my best friend, and the girl I want to spend my time with."

What he said was just perfect, and I told him so. Then Luke said that his granddaddy wanted him second semester to get his grades up, so that a state or community college would be more likely to want him to come and maybe even give him a partial scholarship because of financial need and because both his parents are dead. "Granddaddy also wants me to run cross country next fall to make me well-rounded," he said. Luke told me that his granddaddy felt that if he ran cross country, maybe that would also help him get financial help, too. Luke added that his granddaddy thought he spent too many hours working after school instead of studying and that it might pay off in the long run to play a sport, study more, and work after school much less.

I told Luke that I agreed 100 percent with his granddaddy, that we could work on L&M Enterprises more in the summer and on weekends and less after school and it would be better for both of us. It was one of the best days that Luke and I have ever spent together.

Saturday Night Parties

Chapter Thirty-Seven: Luke

I'd never been to a party before Mia invited me to one at Camila's house for Saturday night. Mia explained that Hannah would be there, too, plus Camila and Hannah's boyfriends, Santiago and Manteo. They're both juniors. I've been invited to parties two other times, once in middle school and once in ninth grade, but I didn't want to go either time. I was so nervous around girls then that I just couldn't stand the thought of being stuck in a corner somewhere and not knowing what to say if some girl did come by to talk to me.

But doing anything with Mia makes me happy. Most everything we've done together has been outdoors, doing stuff like hiking, fishing, and picnics—which are more my kind of things than hers. Besides, it's February and it's cold, and I don't know if it would be fair if I dragged Mia up into the mountains to hike or something. We've been needing to do something anyway that would show that I cared about her and her friends, so I said I'd be glad to come over to Camila's, and Granddaddy said he would be happy to bring me, and I could walk or run home. Obviously, Mia couldn't have the party at her house knowing how her dad thinks about me and that he doesn't even know we're dating. One more month and I'll have my license, and I won't have to rely on Granddaddy all the time to go somewhere. He said I could use his pickup just about any time I needed it.

When Mia asked me to come to the party, one thing that made me really, really happy—when I had time to think about things—was she didn't have to ask—or worry—about me being the only white person there. She knows I don't give a crap about stuff like that. Look, I've been called poor white trash a couple times pretty recently. I hate those words. I'm sick of all those so called "popular" kids looking down on people like me or Hispanic kids. Caleb muttered PWT at me when he hit me from behind at football practice a couple of months ago. He said it just loud enough that I'd hear it, but not so loud that it would be obvious that he said it. Yeah, he's a big, tough dude all right. Thomas used the same slurs when we almost got into it in Ms. Waters' class last month.

And it's not like Mia or me or any of the kids at Camila's party were going to get invited to Caleb's party at his house that same night. His "big bash" that he's been talking about for the past two weeks—Mr. "New 90-inch Widescreen Television." What a jerk.

Mia also didn't have to ask—or worry—about me not liking the Hispanic food that she and the girls were going to come over early and fix. I spent months the beginning of this school year not having enough to eat and worried about when Dad was going to go off and hit me. I'll eat just about anything.

When everybody got to Camila's house, the girls took us downstairs to the basement, and they had everything all ready. They had made chicken fajitas, tomatillo salsa, and this other dish that I forgot what it was called. I liked everything a lot except that salsa dish—that stuff's got a lot of chilies and garlic in it. We had churros for dessert that Mia made. She's made those before for me and they're really good. The last thing we ate—well, everybody except me—was in the "Hot Stuff" contest where everybody else competed to see who could eat the hottest chilies. I got a lot of teasing about not participating, especially from the guys, but I didn't mind. Before it started, I would have bet money that Santiago or Manteo would have won that contest, and sure enough, they finished first and second. After that, we just pretty much sat around and talked and snacked, and the guys and me watched some college basketball games and talked about who was probably going to the Final Four next month. Mia was sitting next to me the whole time and holding my hand most of that time—and really, that alone would have make me happy any day of the week.

I left around nine. I especially didn't want Mia's dad to come pick her up while I was still there. I knew it was going to take more than an hour to walk home, and I didn't want Granddaddy to have to come get me. He's told me he doesn't see so well in the dark anymore when he's driving. I know he's getting old, and I'm worrying more and more about that. And sometimes I confess that I worry about where I would end up if something happened to him since I'm not 18. I mean where would I have gone this year when Mom and Dad died if Granddaddy wasn't around? Would I have gone to a foster home, and where would that have been and would I have had to change schools and then Mia might have been out of my life forever and who would have helped me through geometry and who would I have had to talk to? I've lucked out pretty good this year, compared to how things could have turned out.

When I got home, Granddaddy was asleep in his easy chair with the TV on. He smiled when he saw me and asked about the party and how was Mia, and I said everything was fine. Then he told me he had been calling real estate agents the last couple weeks, and on Sunday, we were going to go driving around looking at land for sale out in the country. He said this would be the best gift he could give me for my future, other than help with college expenses.

Chapter Thirty-Eight: Elly

When Caleb first started talking about the big party he had planned, I was so hoping that he would invite me. I knew he would be there with that awful junior girlfriend of his Rachel, but, still, he at least could see how good I look now, and I might get a chance to talk to him a few times. So I was thrilled when he invited me and not long after that, I got a text from Matthew saying that Caleb had invited him too and that he would pick me up around 6 if that was okay, so I texted back and said that sounded great. Caleb lives on the same street as we do, but I wouldn't have wanted to have walked because it gets so cold now, especially after dark.

Later, I got a text from Mary, saying she had been invited too and was going to go with her new boyfriend Richard, you know, the senior on the football team. I texted Paige to see if she and Allen were going, and she said they had been invited too, but that neither one of them had wanted to go. I was so shocked at that, that I called her and Paige simply said, "Allen and I can't stand Caleb, and we're just going to hang out at my house Saturday night." She knows that I have a thing for Caleb, and I got mad when she said that, but now I wish I hadn't gone to that party at all—the way things turned out.

The party started out all right. Caleb's parents had bought pizzas for us to eat, and we all went downstairs to what Caleb called his "man cave" and we started binge watching *The Walking Dead* and chowing on pizza. But after about an hour of that, Caleb said, "Who's up for some mixed drinks," which made me get really worried. I'd never had alcohol before, and Mom and Dad have told me many times that if I'm out somewhere and other kids are drinking that I'm to have enough courage to not drink. And to call them—no questions asked— to come pick me up if the guy I'm with has been drinking and is getting ready to drive me home. I thought about saying that I didn't care for anything when Caleb started taking orders, but then Mary came back with drinks that she had mixed up for Matthew and me, and it just felt awkward saying that I didn't want anything after she had gone to the trouble of bringing something to me.

The drink just tasted awful, I don't know what was in it, and I can't remember what it was or what Matthew called it. Then about a half later, he brought me another one that was different he said, that it had some vodka in it—I don't remember what else. That drink didn't taste so bad, so I had another one of those later in the evening. I don't remember if I had anything else to drink. Just about everybody was drinking and making out—and Matthew and me were too, and my head was spinning.

Then I remember Matthew saying something about us driving somewhere to have some alone time, and we got in his car, and the next thing I remember was the airbag inflating and slamming me in the face and chest. I felt like my face was bleeding and my right arm hurt like crazy, and I was screaming, then I just passed out. I don't know if it was from the wreck or because I was so drunk. The next thing I remember was waking up at the hospital the next morning and Mom and Dad were there, and Mom said, "Hi, sweetie," and Dad was staring at me with an angry look and didn't say anything for the longest time and then he said the absolute worst thing he's ever said to me and it hurt really bad. He said, "I'm very disappointed in you."

Later that morning, the doctor dismissed me, and on the way home, nobody said anything. I was really stiff and sore, but

I didn't have anything wrong with me except a lot of bruises and abrasions. I slept the rest of the morning and into the afternoon, then my parents "gave me the talk."

The first thing that Dad asked was why Matthew and I were driving in the opposite direction from our house when Caleb's house was only a few houses down the street from ours. I told him I didn't know why. Then he asked, "Were you too intoxicated to know where he was taking you?" All I could say was "Yes, sir," which was the truth. Next he said, "Do to you have any idea what was going to happen when he got to wherever he was going to?" I paused for a long time and then I realized what Dad was suggesting would have happened, and I started crying so bad that I couldn't stop.

Finally Dad said, "As soon as you're able, call or text Matthew and tell him that you two have had your last date and also tell him that you're grounded for at least a month, maybe two." Then he left the room. I started crying again, I was so ashamed and Mom started to hold me and was trying to comfort me, but I couldn't stop crying for the longest time. I hadn't even thought about Matthew since I woke up in the hospital. I should never have gone out with him the first time. We have nothing in common. Why do I keep messing up and making bad decisions when it comes to guys? Why can't I ever get this guy thing right? Later after Mom left my room, I texted Matthew and broke up with him. I didn't call him because I didn't even want to hear the sound of his voice.

Chapter Thirty-Nine: Marcus

"No thank you, we're fine, just give them to somebody else." That's what Kylee told Mary when she brought us some mixed drinks at Caleb's party last Saturday night. I've got to admit that I was a little ticked at first when she said that—that Kylee would make the decision on whether or not we were going to have something to drink. Last year, I know I would have gone off on her over something like that. But the more I thought about things, I was glad she felt comfortable enough in our relationship to speak for the two of us. I fouled up our relationship last year, and I don't want to screw things up again.

Before I left home, Dad and Mom both told me that I was not to have any alcohol if any was offered to me. Did they just assume that there was going to be alcohol at Caleb's party? Later, I told Kylee that I was good with her telling Mary that. She gave me this big smile and an even bigger kiss, so that alone made the whole not drinking thing alright. Coach Dell and Coach Henson have both told their players to remember that we are representing not only the school but our sports teams when we are out in public. And to be careful what we do because if we mess up and it gets on the news or social media it will make the whole team look bad because of the actions of a few.

After we finished watching *The Walking Dead*, we started chowing down on pizza. The guys started playing video games and the girls rooting us on, but once just about everybody began drinking, people started acting stupid. I mean Mary was going around flirting with just about every guy, even the ones that had dates; and Leigh started heaving and turning pale, and she had to run off to the bathroom to throw up. Matthew started pawing at Elly, and, man, that girl was totally out of it after just like two or three drinks. It was pathetic. Nobody wanted to do anything except say how good they felt or how drunk they were getting.

Since Caleb only lives a couple doors down from my house, Dad had told me to just walk Kylee home when we were ready to go home, and that I could drive her home with him sitting in the front seat because I won't have my license until next month. I'm tired of not having a license, but at least I don't have to wait much longer and my driving Kylee home, even though Dad was there, was way better than Dad driving Kylee and me to her house, and both of us sitting in the backseat like we were still kids.

Finally, because the party had totally fallen apart, and maybe I was just imagining things, but I thought I smelled some weed, I decided it was time for Kylee and me to walk to my house—and she was down with that. As we were walking home, I saw Matthew and Elly leave too, and he was all over her while he was taking her to his car. Then they got into his car, and I mean they hadn't driven like but 50 yards when Matthew slammed into a parked car, almost head-on. I mean, dude, how messed up was that. It was pathetic.

Kylee and I ran over to the car, and Matthew and Elly were all covered up by the air bag, and Elly was screaming and Matthew just sat there with this dazed, stupid look on his face like he was still driving. I called 911, and it wasn't long before the cops and the rescue squad were there. Kylee and I stayed by the side of the car, but we were afraid to try to get Matthew and Elly out of the car. Supposed they were injured or something, Kylee said we could have made things worse by moving them.

Mom and Dad came over to us while we were watching Matthew and Elly being pried out of the wreck and put into the rescue squad van. Dad asked me what happened with this real sharp tone in his voice, but after a while, he could tell that Kylee and I had nothing to do with it and that neither one of us had been drinking.

When Dad was driving us to Kylee's house, he told Kylee and me how proud he was of us for our quick thinking at the scene of the accident. And when we got to Kylee's house, he raved to her parents about how mature the two of us had been about the whole thing and then he told Kylee's dad what a fine daughter she had, and her old man said he was real pleased with her choice for a boyfriend. On the way home, Dad kept praising me for being so much more mature, and he went on so long that it got embarrassing. But then I remembered last year when he was on my case all the time, so then getting so much praise didn't seem so bad after all.

When we got back to school on Monday, Coach Henson said at practice that Matthew wouldn't be able to play in our Tuesday or Friday night games, but he hoped he would be back by the playoffs. He didn't have to tell us whether it was because Matthew had hurt himself in the accident or had been suspended from the team for a week. It didn't matter which, it was obvious that Matthew had let the whole team down one way or the other. We barely won the Tuesday night home game against a team we should have blown away. Then we got blown out on Friday night when the guy Matthew would have been guarding went off for 25 points. Man, he really let us down.

Chapter Forty: Mia

I was nervous all day Saturday about Camila's party that night. I was scared that Luke's granddad would drop him off the same time that Poppa dropped me off, or that Poppa would come in and talk to Camila's poppa and somehow find out that Luke was going to be there. Or that some kind of way, Poppa would find out that Luke and I have been dating. Finally, I told Mama about what was bothering me—she said she could tell something was wrong all morning—and Mama told me just to call Luke and tell him to get to Camila's really early or really late, it didn't matter which, and that would solve everything. So I thought the thing to do was to tell Luke to get there at exactly 7, which was the time the party was to start, and I would stall around at home and pretend that I couldn't make up my mind about what to wear and make sure that Poppa and I didn't leave until 7… so that was my plan.

Mama said that was a good plan, but she added that doesn't solve the long-term problem of what we are going to do when Poppa does find out about Luke and me. "Sooner or later," she said, "you know your father, he's going to try to set you up with some boy through his father, and that boy is going to say something like 'Mia already has a boyfriend, Luke,' and that boy's father is then going to relay that information to your Poppa." And then, she said, Poppa was going to throw an absolute fit at both her and me.

I know all that is probably—more than probably, likely—true but I don't want to think about it. So many times, we've been eating dinner on a Friday or Saturday night, and I just wished that Luke could be there; and for Poppa to see what a good person Luke is and for them to get to know each other and for Poppa to find out that Luke really, really has a lot of potential. But then I remember last spring when Luke and I were working behind the house after school and Poppa wouldn't even let him eat at the kitchen table with us. When I think about all those things, my stomach just starts hurting really bad because I worry that Poppa would make me break up with Luke if he ever finds out about us.

Luke and I decided to count the party date as our six-month anniversary of us going out. But I feel like we've been together even longer, ever since he held my hand for the first time on that snow day last winter. I was hoping that he would remember when our six-month anniversary would be without me telling him, and he did. In fact, he brought the subject up and it made me so happy that he is the type of boy that remembers those types of things. Luke and I are both so tight with our money. We both seem so scared all the time that we're never going to have any money to spend on each other. I just don't want poverty to be constantly in the back of my mind. I don't want to live my whole life like that. I don't care about being rich, like some of the kids are like Elly, Mary, Marcus, and Caleb, but I don't want to live my life having these fears that there isn't enough money to get by, especially if some family member got sick or we had a car accident or some kind of disaster happened.

So Luke and I talked things over about what kind of present we could get for each other, and at last we decided that we would give each other a hand-made anniversary card telling five things each—and no more than that—about what we liked best about the other person. And we would give the cards to each other not long after we arrived at Camila's house.

I thought for three days about what I should write on Luke's card and finally the words all just sort of gushed out. The five things were that Luke is kind, that he is sweet to me, and faithful, and that he respects me, and that he is really smart—except in math. I actually wrote "except in math" on his card, and I thought it would make him laugh when he read it—and it did—he just bellowed out a laugh, he thought it was so funny.

Then he gave me my anniversary card. And in it he wrote that I had changed his life for the better, that seeing me always made him smile and feel good about himself, that I was his best friend, that just holding my hand made his day, and that I was just as beautiful on the inside as I was on the outside. I teared up when I read that last thing and then we kissed each other for the longest time, and I didn't care that everybody at the party saw that.

Poppa had said he was going to pick me up at 10:00 that night, that he didn't want me falling asleep at mass the next morning, so I told Luke that he had better leave Camila's around 9:40. When Luke left, he gave me another long kiss; it was just the best night ever.

Never Would
Have Thought

Chapter Forty-One: Luke

I never would have thought that the first girl I would be driving somewhere with alone in Granddaddy's truck would have been Elly, but that's just what happened on Thursday night. The same week I got my driver's license, our school had a first round regional tournament game at home. Ms. Hawk said that she wanted Elly and me to cover the basketball game with Elly taking pictures and me interviewing players, cheerleaders, and students about what it was like for the school to go to its first tournament game in years. Elly told me that her father had to work late at the office that night and her mom had to take her brothers to karate practice, and she said she had asked her mom if I could take her to the game and Elly's mom had said okay.

I can believe that she asked her mom instead of her dad. Her dad looks down on me, I can tell from the way he looks at me and watches me when I come over to mow their lawn. He just looks grim and his face has this sour, pained expression like he has been eating raw lemons all day. It's like if he doesn't keep a close eye on me, I'm going to steal something. Yeah, what would I steal from him while I'm mowing—grass clippings or dandelions or something. Not that her mom probably also wasn't real pleased for me to have to pick Elly up. Everybody at school knows about the wreck that Elly and Matthew were in last month, and how Elly's parents made her break up with him. I don't hold that against them, Matthew is nothing but a cocky jock jerk. So, Elly doesn't have a boyfriend right now to drive her to the game; I guess she's still grounded.

Thanks to Mia and the self-confidence she has given me, I wasn't all twisted up in knots being with Elly, like I would have been with any girl in the past, but especially Elly. When Elly and I left her house, I went over what kind of interviews Ms. Hawk wanted me to get done and how Elly and I were to work together—that kind of stuff. But Elly just nodded her head a little and hardly said anything. She had this weird look on her face. It's only about a 15-minute drive from her house to school, and I was trying to get some feedback from her about how we were going to handle the pictures and interviews, and she still wasn't talking much, so finally I asked her if she was alright.

She blurted out no and teared up a little bit. Then she said, "I haven't been in a car with a boy since the accident and Dad said," and her voice sort of tailed off.

And I said, "Daddy said, 'You'd better be careful with Luke in the car with you—better keep an eye on him,' something like that right?"

"Oh, yes, how did you know?" she said, and then she teared up again.

I'm sick and tired of people like Elly's dad treating me like I'm scum just because of my dad's past and that my parents didn't have much money. I hate that type of attitude crap! I've lost my mom and my dad this year, my grades are okay except for Geometry, and I'm still standing and doing alright. And I've got a great girlfriend and am going to college, and I'm going to be somebody someday. I know I've got a gigantic chip on my shoulder about my family and no money crap, but I'm doing the best I can.

So I said to Elly, "I wouldn't treat you like that. I wouldn't cheat on Mia. I've known you like forever, you can trust me."

"You're right, you wouldn't," and then Elly added, "I feel much better, thank you, let's get to work planning this whole thing out."

And we did. I've got to tell you this journalism thing was exciting. Elly and I had gotten special permission from Coach Henson to come into the locker room before tip-off to do interviews and take pictures. I asked questions like, "What are your thoughts about heading into the school's biggest game in years" and "Are you feeling any pressure." I felt like a professional journalist and Elly was snapping pictures of everybody I was talking to. Then we went to talk to some of the cheerleaders. I know who Leigh is from being in a bunch of classes with her, so I started with her and then we talked to the senior co-captains. Last, we went into the bleachers and talked to students from every class to get their thoughts, and that was neat, too.

Then the game started, and, wow, it was something. Elly and I got to sit under our basket just past the out of bounds marker, and it was amazing seeing all the action so close up. Jefferson has a really good team, but Marcus and Quintin were fantastic and dealing all night. On one of the possessions, Matthew drove the lane, got fouled, and landed really close to Elly and she got this awful look on her face. I don't know what happened before or after that wreck she was in with Matthew, but it must not have been any good.

No team led by more than three points the whole game, and with us up by one point with 15 seconds to go, Marcus stole the ball and was going in for a slam and a three-point lead when one of Jefferson's guards caught up with him and just hacked him from behind. Marcus was in mid-air when it happened and he lost control of the ball and fell awkwardly. His right leg bent funny and his head hit the floor, too. Marcus was on the floor, just writhing in pain and when he tried to stand up, he collapsed again. Coach Henson rushed out on the floor and checked on Marcus, and I could tell from the look on his face that the injury was bad.

The refs should have called a flagrant foul on that Jefferson punk, but they didn't and Marcus was too hurt to shoot free throws, so Quintin had to. He made the first, but the second rimmed out and Jefferson came down and hit a trey at the buzzer to win the game. The crowd was in an ugly mood because a flagrant foul wasn't called and then things really got ugly and people were screaming and cursing at the refs. The parents were much worse than the students.

Elly and I stopped at Dairy Queen to get some ice cream on the way home since she wanted some. We talked non-stop there and all the way home about the game and the work we had done. When we got to her house, she said something that made me feel good, "Thanks for being my friend." I was glad to maybe have helped her out a little.

Chapter Forty-Two: Elly

I never would have thought that Luke would ever have pulled up to my house at night to take me somewhere, but that's what happened Thursday night for a tournament basketball game. Of course, I never thought I would be skinny enough to wear a mini-skirt this year and have guys asking me out. I'm just as miserable now that I'm thin as I was when I was overweight and had to wear those awful glasses. I'm probably more depressed at times, like right now.

I haven't had a date since Matthew and I broke up. Of course, I'm on week four of being grounded and not being allowed to date, though I think Mom and Dad are about ready to let me have a life again. When Ms. Hawk told Luke and me that she wanted us to cover the basketball game on Thursday, I knew I was going to have to ask Luke to take me because Mom and Dad are always tied up on Thursday nights. I was afraid to talk to Dad about it, so I went to Mom and she said she would have to ask Dad about how he would feel about me going with Luke. I begged her not to do that, that going with Luke wasn't a date, that Ms. Hawk had assigned me to the game, and it was for a grade. But all Mom said was that she wasn't so sure how Dad would feel about my being out at night, even though it wasn't a date, with a boy like Luke. Not that she had anything against Luke, he always does "such a nice job, mowing the lawn, you know."

She does have something against Luke, though, I can tell. Wednesday evening at supper, Dad told me that I could go with Luke to the game, but I had to keep an eye on him in case "he pulled anything" and to text him when I got to school and when I left. And that if I "had any doubts whatsoever about riding home with him," to call him and he would come get me.

I had all that nonsense rolling around in my head when I got into the car, that I just couldn't talk with Luke about anything. It's not like I've had much chance to talk about anything when I've been in a car with guys. All the guys I've dated have been so self-centered about their stupid sports and other stupid stuff—it's like I've just been along for the ride—a really boring ride.

But with Luke it was different. He kept talking to me and asking my opinion about what questions he should ask and what kind of pictures I wanted to take, and then he started talking about school and asked what did I think about Mr. Wayne's explanation on the "little known reasons why America won the Revolutionary War." Things like the British coming down with malaria and small pox and their not having the "home court advantage." Then he talked about Mrs. Kendel recommending that he and Mia read *Fahrenheit 451* for their next Friday book club novel and how it seemed really good so far, and he kept going on and on.

So by the time we got to the game, I was talking to him and expressing my opinion on everything, and he was nodding his head and replying and really listening to me. I'm not used to boys being like that; I don't think they know how to act—at least the ones I've been around. Then when we sat down against the wall in the gym to take pictures, I had to sit real close to him and our legs and shoulders touched because there were ball boys and cheerleaders on both sides of us. All these feelings that I have for him every now and then started rushing in, and I knew I had to get control of my emotions before I did something stupid. I would never flirt with Luke because of him and Mia being together, and I have too much respect for Mia to do that anyway because she's really my best friend now. But, still...I get these feelings.

I don't like to watch sports—any sport—but, I've got to say that by the end of the game, I was even excited. The game was so close and the crowd was yelling and cheering like crazy, and nobody really knew who was going to win. When the game had just a few seconds left, Marcus went in to—whatever they call it when a guy jumps real high and he's trying to get real close to the basketball goal and shove the ball into the net—do one of those type things. When Marcus was getting ready to do that, this Jefferson guy knocked Marcus down and hurt him really bad. It was just sickening to see Marcus lying like that on the floor and being hurt so bad. I was so shook up that I forgot to take pictures, but I don't think running pictures in the yearbook of Marcus being hurt would have been a good thing anyway.

On the way home, I told Luke that I was hungry and would he mind stopping and getting an ice cream cone, and I told him I would buy him one, too. He said he would be glad to stop for me, but he didn't want anything to eat. I realized right then that I had probably said the wrong thing, that by what I was saying and the way I said it, I was implying that he was too poor to buy himself ice cream. But, honestly, what I was trying to do was spend a little more time with him. Except for Marcus getting injured and us losing the game, it was the best time I've ever had with a boy, and it wasn't even a date. Maybe I should try to be friends with a guy before I go out with one. Things sure aren't working out with the way I've been going about dating.

Chapter Forty-Three: Marcus

I never would have thought that I would get injured playing basketball. It was getting hurt on a football field that was always in the back of my mind. But that's what happened Thursday night in the first game of regionals. We had a great season. Coach Henson told us after we won our league regular season and league tournament titles that we were his best team in the 12 years he's been coaching varsity. After we won our conference tournament game, coach told me to come into his office and he said that he was really pleased with my progress as a player, but most of all, he really appreciated how I had become a better teammate and leader this year... that I was becoming a man.

His praise really meant a lot to me. I realize now that I was a jerk most of my freshman year on the football and basketball teams, and maybe getting caught cheating in history class and getting punished at home and at school was the best thing that ever has happened to me. Coach Henson told me that the thing that impressed him most about my sophomore season was that I was second on the team to Quintin in assists with 4.2 per game—that's "excellent," he said, "for a high school shooting guard." Last year, I was only concerned about what my scoring average was, but now I really like dishing out those assists.

The regional game was at home because we had earned it because of our regular season and league tournament success. I really thought we were going to win because of the home court advantage, but everybody on the team knew that Jefferson was no pushover. The game started out great. Quintin fed Matthew for a fast break layup right off the tip, and I drained a three at the end of the quarter to put us up by five. At halftime, we were up by six points and everything was looking great. Maybe we were already thinking that we would be playing in the next round at home on Saturday night.

Still, we stayed solid in the third quarter and we were ahead by seven points at the start of the last quarter, but then the wheels just seemed to come off. Jefferson hit a trey to start the quarter, then right after that Matthew got a technical called on him for cursing about a travelling call that went against him. Jefferson got two free throws and possession after that and they turned that into four points and all of a sudden, they were just down one. Maybe we panicked a little after that because we went cold from the field for three minutes and we were down by four before we knew what had hit us.

We were still down by four with two minutes left in the game when I hit a three, then we had a stop; and on our next possession, I fed Quintin for a backdoor layup and all of a sudden we were up by one. We even got the rebound on Jefferson's next possession, but couldn't take advantage of it when Matthew lost the ball going in for a layup. I thought he was fouled but the refs didn't call anything, and Quintin had to separate Matthew from one of the refs, he was jawing at him so hard. Maybe we should have kept our minds on the game instead of worrying about how the officials were calling things.

What happened next, I'm still a little foggy about. I picked Jefferson's pocket when their shooting guard went behind his back. I thought I had a clear path to the basket for a dunk that would have put us up by three with less than 15 seconds left. When I was skying toward the rim, I got hit from behind and when I landed, I fell funny and I knew my right leg was hurt real bad. And my head hit the floor, too.

I remember rolling around on the floor in pain, but that's about it. I must have passed out because the next thing I knew I was in the emergency room and still feeling groggy and in pain and Coach Henson and Mom and Dad and Joshua had their heads down and then I knew we had lost. I don't even want to know what the final score was or what happened after I left the game. My right leg was hurting so bad, and I kept passing out and people kept telling me to wake up.

Later, I found out that I had a torn ACL and a mild concussion. I can live with the concussion, that's no big deal. But the ACL thing means that I'm going to miss spring football practice and not be able to play any pickup basketball this summer… my leg's going to take four to six months to heal said the doctor. The worst case scenario is that I only miss a couple of football games at the start of the season. I got to admit that I'm worried sick about my coming back and having the speed and quickness that I once did. I mean, that's always been the best part of my game. If I lose those two things, I can't be a wide-out anymore. I don't want to have to gain 30 pounds and become a tight end like Joshua. Then I also wouldn't have the speed and quickness like I need to have to be a shooting guard.

I couldn't get my leg surgery scheduled until Monday and my leg didn't hurt too bad because of the painkillers, but I was still so dizzy I spent Friday and Saturday just sitting around the house. Kylee came by after school and visited and spent much of the day Saturday at my house. I really appreciated that, her doing that made me feel close to her. Coach Henson and a bunch of the guys on the basketball team also came over and visited me Friday right after school, but Caleb didn't come by even though he just lives down the street. We're not solid anymore. I guess he figures he's going to have a new number one receiver next year anyway. I'll show him, though.

Chapter Forty-Four: Mia

I never would have thought that Luke, Elly, Marcus, and I would be in the same room alone together at Marcus' house, but that's what happened last Saturday morning. I had to babysit in Elly's neighborhood on Friday night, so earlier in the week she said when I was done why not walk down the street and spend the night at her house? She said we could binge watch Netflix or Hulu or something and make fudge and eat that while watching and talking and so on until we were too tired to stay up. Luke and I had planned an afternoon date for Saturday afternoon, because he had to till somebody's garden and plant their fruit trees on Saturday morning, so he and I decided that he could just pick me up at Elly's when he was done with the job.

But after Marcus was injured at the basketball game on Thursday night, I suggested to Luke and later to Elly that the three of us go visit him after Luke finished work. I reminded Luke that Marcus and his brother stood up for him that time he got injured at football practice and Luke owed it to Marcus to come by and see how he was doing. Luke agreed and said I was right. That's one of the reasons why I like Luke so much; he listens to me and respects what I have to say. I've heard Elly, Camila, and Hannah and lots of other girls say that one of the major problems they are having with guys is that they won't listen to common sense suggestions. That if the guy doesn't come up with the idea to do something or change something about himself, then we can just forget about it happening.

Mary says the trick is to get a guy to think that it was his idea first and then praise him for having thought of the change we want him to make before he actually ever does it, let alone think about it. Maybe Mary is right that we have to con a guy into doing something, but I don't want a guy like that in the first place. I really don't care much for Mary, to be honest. I don't trust her. I hate it that I think that way about another girl, but it's true.

I really had a good time at Elly's house Friday night. She told me all about Luke and her covering the game Thursday night and that he had really come out of his shell since his freshman year and several times he raved about how great I was. That made me feel really good; I'm so glad he's my boyfriend. I'd heard so much talk about how great Netflix and Hulu and binge-watching some show are that I was glad that I finally got to see what all the fuss was about. But honestly, I don't get the point of watching some show for hours and hours. It just seemed like such a waste of time. Elly and I watched some stupid show about dead people walking around half crazy and weird, then I told her why not just turn the thing off and we could talk until we were sleepy and full of fudge... so that's what we did until around 2. I've never been up that late in my life, but I still woke up at 6 because that's what time I have to get up every day to do chores and take care of the chickens. I just couldn't go back to sleep, so I got out *Sand County Almanac*, one of the books that Luke wanted me to read about the outdoors, until Elly finally woke up around 9:00. I confess that I started rustling around in the room and making noise. I think she would have slept until noon.

Luke came over at 10:00 when we were finishing breakfast, and I could tell that he was hungry because he had been up so long and working so hard. I know that he appreciates it when I look out for him... he's told me so. So Elly and I made him an egg sandwich and then we walked down the street to Marcus' house. Elly had called his mom the night before, so she knew we were coming. I could tell Marcus really appreciated us coming by, and he and Luke talked and talked about the game, analyzing every little thing. Why we had gotten the lead and why we lost the lead, and I really didn't understand what they were talking about, but the two guys were into it.

Then Luke asked Marcus about his leg and how long it would take to heal so he could "get back to being 100 percent." They had a really serious discussion about all that, and I could tell that Marcus was scared about how much he could recover. Marcus was so cocky last year about being a professional athlete that I can understand why he's so worried. He really has grown up a lot since then. But he should be really worried. Because she's a nurse, I asked Mama about how serious a torn ACL is for an athlete, especially somebody like Marcus. She said he might never be the player he once was, of course, depending on a lot of things, especially if he ever reinjures that leg; but on the other hand, he could have a great recovery. Marcus might have all his sports dreams turn out right for him, but the smart thing would be for him to start thinking about a backup plan. I was glad we all went to see him and got to know him better.

Tests
and
More Tests

Chapter Forty-Five: Luke

The other day, Ms. Whitney came into Ms. Hawk's English 10 Honors class and told us that she wanted all of us to take the PSAT 10 next week and how important it was for preparing for the PSATs our junior year and then the SATs. I'd already signed up, I know they're important for me, but, still, I dread taking the thing. At least, it wasn't as bad as the Geometry SOL test was and all the crap I had to go through for that.

Things started off bad and just got worse as the whole process went on. It began when Mrs. Waters told me and most of the class that we had to either come in before school for 45 minutes of tutoring or stay after for it. I chose the before school prison instead of the after school version, so I wouldn't have it hanging over my head all day and so I could get my lawn moving jobs taken care of. Ms. Waters and the other geometry teacher, Mrs. Roberts, were both in there with my fellow losers from their two classes and one of the kids in my group was Thomas. I've tried to stay away from him ever since we almost got into it earlier in the year, and when he came into tutoring (predictably he was late) he walked by my desk and whispered, "Sooner or later, I'm gonna beat the crap out of you." Of course, he didn't use the word *crap* if you know what I mean. I thought about saying something smart right back at him, but I decided to just let it slide. I don't know if I could take him one on one in a fair fight. What's the difference anyway who wins or loses; if we get into a fight, we'll both get suspended. So when he stared at me to see what kind of reaction I was going to give him, I just shrugged. I guess I'll worry about fighting him if and when it happens. High school boy fights are mostly pushing and shoving and lots of threats. But, gosh, when high school girls fight it's absolutely vicious: hair pulling, biting, scratching, and cursing, that hair pulling especially is insane.

Then Mrs. Roberts started going over some standard SOL questions with Thomas, me, and two other math losers. The first one was very easy said Mrs. Roberts, "It's about functions, and you all remember what they are." No, I don't; I remember the word *function* and that there are variables and inputs and outputs, then long lines of numbers after the directions and the next thing is a list of multiple answers—or multiple guesses—then the wrong answer that I just penciled in the blank comes next. I missed the easy "sample question," and so did Thomas and one of the other math losers in our group. You know you're in a remedial class, when three out of the four participants can't get the sample question right.

Mrs. Roberts should have stopped right there and gone back over functions because it was clear that 75 percent of her group had forgotten what they were—or never knew. But she apparently was on a schedule, so we rushed on to the next debacle. It had to do with Venn diagrams, which are these circles that have bled into each other with words like *isosceles* and equilateral hovering nearby like a flock of vultures waiting to pick your bones. All four of us got the sample question wrong on that one. But good old Mrs. Roberts seemed unflustered by her young scholars' stupidity and kept on going to a ratio sample question which had to do with the ratio of a slope to a line that answered to the name of *J* and something was parallel to the line J or maybe it intersected the J or ran through it, who knows, who cares, who is gonna use this stuff in real life? Maybe I should have told good old Thomas right about then to beat the snot out of me and put me out of my misery.

And so it went until the bell for first period mercifully rang. I had a week of before-school tutoring like that and I still failed the geometry SOL with a 375. Ms. Waters after she gave me the news on that one told me that since I had failed the SOL with such a high number (400 is passing) I had the opportunity to take "expedited retakes" in two days. I could tell how hard she was trying to convince me that this was a good thing, but all I could see was that I had another "opportunity" to look stupid to her.

Two days later, after more before school tutoring, I took the expedited retake and made a 395—just five points from passing and once again, Ms. Waters said I had earned the opportunity to have another expedited retake. When is this crap ever going to end? Then I remembered last year on the Algebra I SOL, that I just Christmas treed the whole test, putting A, then B, then C, then D in those blanks and then going D, C, B, and A on the next round. And I passed the SOL with that approach. But I got to thinking that I wouldn't luck out that way twice, I mean that really was a freak way to pass a math test. So on the third geometry SOL test, I decided to answer the questions I thought I might know with my best guess, then on the ones that I didn't know and had narrowed the answer down to two possibilities, I would write in the letter that I didn't think was the answer. My reasoning was that since I had already failed the thing twice, and those sadistic math teachers that create this crap are trying to fool us into putting down the wrong answer, I would put down what I thought was the wrong answer and it might be right. Does that make any sense at all?

Well, anyway, I don't know what the heck happened, but when my SOL scores came back the third time, I had made a 405, which meant that not only had I passed the SOL but also I had clinched passing Geometry for the year. Man, there's no way that Ms. Waters is going to fail me now and risk having me next year in her room. By the state and the school, I am now officially and statistically "proficient" in geometry... what a joke. I swear, I think some of the people who run things care more about students being "proficient" than us actually learning something we can use in life.

Chapter Forty-Six: Elly

I had a really, really good week last week; maybe my life is beginning to turn around. It started on Monday when I took the geometry SOL and only missed two questions on the whole test. The only person in my advanced class that scored better was Mia and, of course, she had a perfect score.

I also was finally old enough to get my driver's license, and Mom and Dad said because I had truly been sorry about the "party episode" and had been trying to be more responsible and mature, that I was no longer grounded. Of course, my doing so well on the geometry SOL didn't hurt my cause. Then they said they had a surprise for me, and we went out to the garage. When I had gotten home from school, I was wondering why Mom's car was parked out on the street. Usually, Mom parks her car in the garage and when Dad gets home, he leaves his out by the curb. Dad's got so much lawn care stuff and woodworking materials on his side of the garage that there's no room for his car.

Dad rolled up the garage door and inside was a baby blue Prius. For a second or two, I wondered what was that strange car doing in there, but then I realized it was for me! It's not brand new, it's three years old, said Dad, but it has low mileage and should be just fine for me. "Maybe, that can still be your car when you go away to college," said Mom.

"I'd be very okay with that," I told them both and then I gave both my parents a big hug, and said I really appreciated them and would try not to let them down again. I really meant that. I started texting all my friends to let them know about my grounding being over and the Prius, and Mary texted back and said she would spread the word about my "being back among the living." She will, too, she's such a gossip.

About an hour later, I got a text from this senior Eric, who I only know just barely from the monthly Spanish Club meeting, and said he was glad to hear about my "newfound freedom." I texted back "thank you," and then for the next couple hours we texted back about every 10 minutes about some little thing. I'm not stupid, I knew what he was trying to do… figure out if I was showing enough interest in him to ask me out. He's not bad looking, I don't know what his grades are like; he seems okay, but I barely know him. It's April and the prom's next month and I bet he doesn't have a date. Didn't I say just recently that it's better to be friends with a boy first before dating him? But, again, the prom's next month, and I don't have a date. But I'm only a sophomore and have two more years I can go to the prom. On the other hand, I went to the prom as a freshman, and it would be a shame not to go as a sophomore.

Predictably, Eric came by my lunch table the next day and hung around and hung around and was talking about just general stuff. It was so obvious that he was working himself up to ask me out, but he didn't quite have the confidence to do it. I was smiling a lot and trying to make eye contact with him, but he kept looking off into to the distance or looking down and studying his shoes and finally he just drifted off to where he had been sitting. Mary came by—we don't sit together at lunch anymore, she sits with some junior and senior girls and guys—to where Paige and I were sitting, and she said the word was that Eric was going to ask me out to the prom. Sure enough, he texted me that night and asked me to the prom, and I tried to play it cool and not text back for half an hour so as to sort of let him know that I was thinking about it or had a lot of people texting me and guys asking me out. But instead, I texted back in, like, 12 minutes and wrote, "That would be fantastic!!!"

But I didn't feel fantastic about agreeing to go to prom with him. Instead, I sort of felt blah and like I had let myself down again. Does that make sense, I don't know. I told Mom about the prom date and she said she was excited for me, but then she looked me in the eye and said, "But you don't seem that excited."

I forced this big smile and started talking about what a great guy Eric is and how smart he is, but I don't really know if all that is true or not. Mom said she and I would go prom dress shopping on Saturday and pick out something really pretty, and that I could drive the Prius to the mall and we would have lunch out later—"A girls' day out," she exclaimed. I gave a sincere smile to that, but I just worry that I've made another mistake involving guys.

Later that night, I called Mia and let her know all about my news, and we talked for a while and then she suggested that I could drive her home from school and have dinner at her house and then drive to the library to study for the PSAT 10 test. I told her I couldn't imagine either one of us needing to study very much for that test, but then she confessed—and she said she was ashamed to admit it—but that what she really wanted for us to do was try to convince Luke to meet us at the library that night and work on his "math deficiencies" so he would do better on the PSAT. I said I would be glad to drive her to the library and help her tutor Luke.

Chapter Forty-Seven: Marcus

I keep having headaches and my leg still hurts after the ACL surgery, and it seems like the doctors keep giving me tests and more tests. Something's just not right somewhere. I was supposed to take the PSAT 10 test earlier this week, but the test was in the morning and that's when the headaches are worse, and Mom told me not to take the test if I wasn't at my best, which I'm not so I just stayed at home that morning and went to my afternoon classes. The first four or five days I was back in school after my surgery I only went half days anyway; sometimes I went to my morning classes and other days I went to the afternoon ones. My grades are suffering, but Mom and Dad are really understanding, especially Mom. She has this worried look on her face all the time when she's around me, and she's, like, staring intently at me all the time.

Ms. Hawk has been really nice to me, too. One day she called me to her desk when the bell rang and told me to drop by her room after I finished eating lunch—that she wanted to talk to me. She then reassured me that my coming by wasn't for anything bad, which relieved me because I've been so spacy I thought that I might have forgotten to have done some paper or something. Anyway, when I got to her room after eating, she asked about my recovery and we talked about that for a while and she said, "I want you to know how proud I am of your improvement in your writing skills this year and your overall effort. I believe you'll recover just fine from your injuries, but even if you don't, I believe you'll have a bright future."

I thanked her for all that, it meant a lot to me for her to say what she said; I haven't had a lot of good news lately. But then I asked her, and I wasn't being sarcastic, about what on earth would I do if I couldn't play professional sports and go into broadcasting after I retired from playing?

She said "Lots of things, how about going into sports medicine, or being a coach, or maybe even teaching." I laughed when she said all that, but she was real serious and explained what she had meant. She said the head and leg injuries I had had would give me an understanding of what other people went through when they had those and other injuries, and maybe during my recovery process, I could talk to doctors and athletic trainers about what made their jobs worthwhile to them. That answer really made me think. I know, I just know, that I'm going to be alright, but it wouldn't be bad for me to pump those doctors and trainers about my condition and how other people recovered from the things I'm dealing with, and why those doctors and trainers went into medicine.

So I told her, the sports medicine thing was something I could see being interested in and maybe doing, but I said no way would I want to go into coaching high school athletes. She said I would be great at that, too, and I disagreed with her. Then she said, "From what I've heard, you haven't been exactly the most coachable player, especially in the ninth grade, right?" I said yeah to that, but that I had changed and she said my past screw-ups and my newfound maturity would help me relate to high schoolers and also give me stories to tell about how I had had to grow up and show more maturity and why they should, too. Everything she said made sense and made me once again realize what a loser I had been last year. No wonder I was having relationship problems and girls kept dumping me.

Next, we talked about the possibility of a teaching career, which made no sense at all to me when she brought it up. But she said that I might really enjoy teaching history—she knew how good I was in that—or my teaching health and phys ed would fit in well if I decided to go into coaching. I then got a little sarcastic with her and asked, "What about me teaching English?"

She said—and she smiled when she answered, "I don't think the world is quite ready for that, stick to history or phys ed," and we both laughed.

That Friday night, Kylee came by and picked me up and we went out to dinner. I'm old enough to drive finally, but Mom and Dad won't let me for obvious reasons. It was hard at first having a girl come by my house and pick me up and do all the driving, but Kylee has been so sweet about the whole thing that it's been okay. At dinner, I told Kylee all about my conversation with Ms. Hawk, and she was down with the suggestions. She thought I would be a success at any of those possible jobs, and she could see me enjoying them. Kylee also said that she was sure I was going to have a full recovery from both my injuries and that she would continue to be there for me to talk to and run things by. I felt really close to her that night and am really glad we're together.

Chapter Forty-Eight: Mia

I am tired of all these SOL tests and preparing for them non-stop in most of my classes. The tests are so easy, they're so boring. What I like best about school is learning new things and being challenged about things that have questions but no easy answers to them. Or doing projects or researching something that I want to learn more about. Most of the SOL tests just have multiple choice questions, and they don't require me to think deeply about anything. I'm not going to have multiple choice tests when I'm an adult, but I am going to have to think deeply about hard things and big ideas.

The best part of my life is spending time with Luke. Anything we do, anywhere we go, it's so great to talk to him and ask him for his opinions on things and then have him listen to mine and have him comment on them. I confess to scheming so I can spend more time with him. The other day I invited Elly to come over to my house for dinner and then afterwards for us to go to the library and tutor Luke in the math section of the PSAT 10 test. Yes, I wanted to tutor him, and yes I really enjoy spending time with Elly, but also I just wanted to be with Luke for a little while at night, even if was tutoring him in math.

This is the second time Elly has come over for dinner. Last year, Poppa wanted to have what he considered American dishes, but this time, Mama and I decided that we would have a traditional Mexican dinner, so we decided on corn tortillas stuffed with beef, onions, and peppers. It was really good, and

Elly really enjoyed it. Earlier, I had told Mama that Elly and I were going to meet Luke at the library for tutoring after dinner, and she said that would be fine. I know she likes Luke—she's told me so many times and she is sincere. But, sometimes I just wish I could announce at the dinner table one evening that, "My boyfriend Luke is coming over to dinner tomorrow night, and he's going to kiss me good night when he leaves, and, Poppa, there is nothing in the world wrong with that!" Instead, I have to sneak around to meet him, and I'm sick of all that.

Poppa keeps asking if I'm dating anyone and wanting to know why I never want to go out with all the Hispanic guys he keeps offering to set me up with because he's friends or acquaintances with their dads. I'm sick and tired of all that, too. Mama just sits there quietly when all that is going on, and I have to stare at my sisters when Poppa is going on and on about some boy that would be perfect for me. I'm surprised my sisters haven't told Poppa about Luke, even if it were by accident.

When Elly and I got to the library, I saw Luke was already there in his pickup, and he practically jumped out of his car to come greet me. We hadn't seen each other in maybe three hours, but every time we're together it just seems like... magic! The three of us then went to a table at the back of the library and started the tutoring process. On the way over to the library, Elly and I decided that the best way to help Luke was to go to one of those sample tests online and help him learn how to select the best answer. The way I think the SOL tests work is that there are four possible answers: one of which is obviously wrong and stupid, a second that looks wrong after you think about it for a couple seconds, and third and fourth answers that are really similar to each other, but one of them is still clearly the better answer of the two.

But Luke is so weak in math, he can't even pick out the obviously wrong answer until he studies it for a long time. When he finally does figure out that part of the question, he can't seem to understand which one of the other three questions can't possibly be right, let alone figure out which one of the last two questions isn't the answer. Elly and I stayed at the library and worked with Luke for almost an hour, and, honestly, I don't think we helped him enough for him to do well on the math part of the PSAT 10.

Sure enough, when the results came out, he had great scores in the reading and writing sections and really low marks in the math part. I don't care if Luke is not any good in math, he's a good person with a good heart—that's what means the most to me. After the three of us finished with the tutoring, we stopped at an ice cream parlor and ate our cones and talked in Elly's car until it was time to go home. We all had the nicest time talking about school and life and current events, just anything and everything. Elly announced that she has a new boyfriend and they had their first date last Friday night, so that neither one of them would have "first date anxiety when we go to the prom," said Elly.

I doubt that Luke and I ever will go to a prom together. Neither one of our families could ever afford it anyway. Besides I can have a great time with Luke on a Thursday night at the library and at an ice cream parlor—who needs all that glitz and glamor and high school drama that goes along with going to a prom.

Do Clothes Make the Boy— or Girl?

Chapter Forty-Nine: Luke

I've been wanting to take Mia out at night to somewhere special, and we've been talking about where to go and all that. I told her that I wanted to pay for our whole meal as a way to show how much she means to me, but she wanted to pay for her food because it would be too expensive for me if I paid for both of ours. Then she suggested that why doesn't she pay for mine, and I pay for hers, but then after agreeing on that, we both decided that each of us would be so worried about the cost of everything that neither one of us would order anything expensive.

Finally, we came up with the idea that we would take on some extra job somewhere together and then we would use that money to pay for our dinner out. Next, we couldn't think about anything extra that we could do because it seems like we're studying or going to school all the time and when we're not, she's off babysitting and I'm doing some kind of manual labor. But then just out of nowhere, Leigh's mom contacted Mia through our website and asked if we could dig up her old shrubbery lining the front of the house and plant some holly bushes instead. We worked there from noon until almost dark that Saturday and got it done. I used Granddaddy's pickup to go to the local lawn and garden shop and picked up the hollies on Friday after school so we could work straight through on Saturday.

We worked like dogs all of Saturday afternoon, and we were both hot, sweaty, and filthy dirty. When we were finished,

I put my hot, dirt covered hand in hers and gave it a squeeze, and she put her grimy, sweaty face close to mine and we kissed. So we had our money to go out to eat and Mia thought there would be some left over for us to split to put into our respective bank accounts for college. She's so wonderful!

Then I started worrying about not having anything to wear. All I've got are jeans and two pairs of khaki pants. I've got school jeans that become work jeans when they start to get holes in them. You know that fad about kids buying jeans with holes in them to look stylish? Well, I was styling way before it became a fad. Beats me why some kids would pay extra to have holes in their jeans.

I shared my fear with Mia about not having the right kind of clothes to wear out to a restaurant. She said I would look like her knight in shining armor no matter what I wore. We both thought I should have on a tie, and all I have are some clip-ons from when I was a kid. But then she suggested that I borrow one of my granddaddy's and that problem was solved.

The next "crisis" that we had to solve was where would we meet? Obviously, I couldn't drive over to her house, knock on the door, and tell her father that I was there to pick up his daughter—my girlfriend. Man, that would have been the disaster of all time. Mia is always thinking about things. She came up with the idea that she would tell her mom what we were planning and see if she would write a note to the attendance office that Mia was going to ride the bus over to Camila's house to spend the night. All that would be true, too, because I could pick up Mia there and bring her back there when our date was over, and she really would spend the night there.

Then Mia confessed that she and her mom had sewn a dress during the winter with the hope that she could wear it if we ever went out at night somewhere. That when she and I started planning our night out, she had thought about wearing the dress to school that day. But then she decided that she wanted me to see her in this beautiful new dress for the first time when we were out together. Can't you see how much this girl means to me? She's always looking to please me and make me happy. And I feel like I'm doing the same for her. At least I hope I am. She tells me that I am, so it must be true.

The funny thing was that our date was on the same night as prom was, and we both remembered how we had gone out for ice cream our freshman year on that same night. She then asked if I thought we would want to go to prom together next year and then Mia immediately apologized for being too forward. I told her not to feel that way, that one of the many things I liked about her was that she has a mind of her own and isn't afraid to make suggestions or talk about what the future might bring us. But the more we talked about going to prom together our junior year, the more we both decided that we wouldn't even want to. It's just too much expense for one night and after the prom is over, that money is gone forever with "nothing to show for it," she said. I agreed. Then I said, "Let's go out for ice cream next spring on prom night? What do you think, is it a date?"

And she said that it was, she'd put it on the calendar on her website. She did too. The next day I was looking at our job schedule for the months to come and next May there was already a note, stating "Remember to confirm crucial L&M Enterprise meeting for first Friday night in May."

Chapter Fifty: Elly

I thought Mom and I were going to have a wonderful time shopping for my prom dress, but we spent most of the time at the mall arguing. Things started off bad from the beginning. At the first store, I picked out this awesome short, open-back dress with a low-V neck, and Mom started complaining that it was too short at the bottom and too revealing at the top. That I didn't have to dress that way for boys to notice me, since I'm so thin now. And I told her that I've spent my whole life wearing frumpy, old woman clothes, that I was tired of dressing like that, plus, I'm old enough now to make my own decisions about the clothes that I wear.

Then Mom said something smart, "Says the girl who's never had a full or even a part-time job and who contributes how much money every month to the family's financial affairs?"

I snapped right back that she and Dad "always say that my job is to make good grades so that I can have a good future," and that I'm a straight *A* student "again this year except for a *B* in phys ed and health. Is that not good enough for you to show how responsible I am?"

Mom shot right back with "Says the girl who passed out drunk in the front seat of a car with a boy who was up to no good."

I admit that that last little comment really stung—really hurt—and Mom could see that it hurt me, but by then we were both so mad at each other that neither one of would apologize so we just sort of walked around in icy silence for a while, me looking at prom dresses that were so risqué that even I didn't want to try them on, let alone wear them. But I was stopping to "admire" them just to make her even madder at me, and she kept rolling her eyes and frowning at me, as if she didn't know that I knew what she was doing… and she was the one who was acting immature, not me.

Finally, we came across this solid black dress that was still fairly short but not terribly short or low cut, and I had been examining so many that were so much "worse" to her way of thinking that she probably thought this one wasn't so bad and she said, "That one would be barely acceptable, and I am using the word *barely* literally and figuratively." So that is the one we bought. Then I said I needed new shoes to go with it, and she said, "No, you most certainly do not, use a pair you already have."

I was so stressed out from arguing with her, and I figured I had gotten most of what I wanted and she probably figured she had "won" with the "barely" acceptable dress and the no new shoes declaration, that I just decided to let the shoe thing slide. We had said we were going out for lunch, but by the time we made it to the woman at the check-out register, Mom and I were still not on good terms and those terms were not helped when the woman at the register said, "How wonderful to see, a girl and her mom out shopping together for prom." I rolled my eyes to the lady and I happened to look at Mom at the same time, and she was rolling her eyes, too. What is it with females and eye rolling at each other? Is that our version of fist fighting like the boys do? I don't think Mom and I said ten words to each other on the way home.

Prom night with Eric was a total dud, I mean it was worse than going with Paul last year, if you can believe that… and that was a pretty awful night. This was our second—and half way through the evening I knew—and last date. He never made one comment about my dress or how great I looked. He barely talked at all when we were at the restaurant. When we got to the prom, he held out his sweaty hand to take mine, and all I could think was how gross and slimy his hand was. And that boy simply cannot dance at all, and I kept asking him questions when we were dancing or sitting down, and he kept giving these answers that had nothing to do with what I had asked or talked about and his voice was so low that I couldn't understand him and sometimes couldn't tell that he was even talking except for his lips moving a little. I swear, at least Paul talked all the time, although all he wanted to talk about was himself and sports.

I saw Caleb at the prom and that awful junior he's been dating, and I started visualizing myself with Caleb at the prom this time next year and how glamorous and exciting that would be and how many girls would be jealous of me. And then I thought I was being shallow, and I started hating myself for thinking of Caleb and me being together, and I next realized that while I was doing all that thinking, Eric and I had sat beside each other for like ten minutes, and neither one of us had said anything the whole time, and I knew I didn't care.

We left the prom really early which I was very, very happy to have done, because I couldn't stand being with him anymore. When we got to my house, he said his longest sentence of the evening, "I'll come open the car door for you and walk you to your front door." Which I interpreted to mean that he was going to give me a kiss when we got to the door, and I thought that would be gross and sloppy like his hand, so I said, "No thank you, I can let myself out, thank you for a wonderful time." I practically fled up the sidewalk. What an awful night.

Chapter Fifty-One: Marcus

Finally, in a week, I'll be old enough to drive on my own, and I'm worried that Mom and Dad won't let me. I haven't even driven with Mom since I was injured. I'm still having dizzy spells. The good news is that my leg is healing right on schedule. I still think I will be close to being ready to play football when we start practicing in August. Maybe, I won't be able to practice in pads, but I can go full bore with the weight lifting and maybe the running. I bet my parents are going to tell Coach Dell behind my back that they don't want me doing any contact drills. He's probably going to agree with them, too. Everybody will say it's because they want my leg to be fully healed, but I really bet it's because of the concussion.

I know I mouthed off last fall when Mom and Dad bought me the Fiat, it's still a piece of crap car, but it's beginning to look a lot better... just driving a car—any car—would be better than my parents taking me everywhere or Kylee coming by to pick me up when we go out. Just last Friday, she came by and picked me up so we could go out for pizza. Last year, I felt like I had to take Kylee and those other girls I dated out to a super fine restaurant. That I had to show them how sharp I could dress and impress them with how much money I spent on them at a restaurant. Now, I see that it's okay to wear a pullover shirt and jeans and be out with a girl that just wants to be with me and doesn't care about how much money I spend on her.

Still, sometimes I act like a jerk—like at the start of the date. Things got a little weird when Kylee knocked on the door to pick me up. All she said she liked my "casual look," because she just had on jeans and a blouse. I mean, the guy is supposed to pick up the girl, the guy is supposed to tell the girl how good she looks. I admit I was pretty foul when we got into her car, and she was chatting away and I wasn't saying nothing. Then all of a sudden, she said, "What's the matter, Marcus, you're in a mood. Spill it!" I started to say nothing was the matter, but then I realized saying something like that wasn't going to satisfy her.

She's a strong woman; she knows her own mind and is not going to take crap off anybody... including me. Thinking about it now, because she's that way, that's probably why we broke up last year. Maybe I need a strong woman for a girlfriend, maybe deep down I know that now. Mom's a strong woman; she's not some little wifey-dear that lets Dad make all the decisions. Last year, I never paid any attention to how they operate, now I see how things work between them. If Mom has some sort of opinion or idea about something, she'll lay it all out and present her case to Dad. If he disagrees, he'll go into great detail about what he thinks is best, then she will give her counter-argument. Then they start, I'd guess you call it negotiating, and that goes on for a while. They both usually make some compromises and later come to a decision. Maybe that's how a marriage works, how a relationship with a girl in high school works—that is if a guy wants to stay in a relationship with a girl who knows her own mind.

So instead of snapping at Kylee when she asked me what was wrong, I took this long pause and thought about all that stuff and then told her I appreciated her picking me up and telling me how great I looked dressed up, but, then, suddenly, I asked her to pull over the car and she did. I can't believe what I did next... I started tearing up right in front of her. I mean, I'm a football and basketball player, I'm 16 years old, I'm a guy, and I'm hiding my face in front of a girl. She got this all worried look on her face, unbuckled her seat belt, and reached over to hug me and asked what was wrong. And I did "spill it," like she had told me to.

"I'm worried about these headaches," I said. "I have them every day, sometimes more than once. I'm scared I'm never going to get over them."

"Marcus," she said, "you've got to be patient. Everything will heal, your leg, your headaches will go away. That's what the doctors say, right?"

I said, "Yeah, that's what they say, but what if they're wrong? What if I never play sports again?"

"Look," she said, then she got really deep. "Suppose your leg doesn't heal so that you're all the way back from that injury. Suppose your headaches go away eventually, but the doctors tell you it's too big a risk for you to play sports again. Are you going to be a failure for the rest of your life?"

"No," I said. I guess I said that because it was what she wanted to hear. But my whole life has been wrapped up in sports, and maybe I might not be able to play football or basketball anymore. But I'm not a loser, I come from a good home, I'm not stupid. Yes, my life would not be over if sports was over. But playing ball has always meant just about everything to me. It's who I am.

"Marcus," she said. "I really like you, maybe one day we might even fall in love with each other. Who knows? I do know what kind of guy I want. I want a guy who respects me and my opinion, who wants to be equal to me but not superior. I think maybe you can be that guy or I wouldn't be spending time with you. I wouldn't care if you never played sports again, as far as my wanting to be with you. But if you're happy playing sports, then I would always support you. But I'm a lot more interested in Marcus the man than I'm interested in Marcus the jock."

I mean, man, she absolutely floored me with that type of talk. She started up the car and we went on to go eat. We talked like that all night through dinner and on the way home. It was the best date I've ever had… she's something.

Chapter Fifty-Two: Mia

When Luke picked me up at Camila's house for our first "nighttime" date, the first thing I noticed about him was that he had on a pair of light blue pants with a dark green shirt and a tie that didn't match either one of them. Luke has zero fashion sense, and you know what, I could care less. Clothes don't make the man—a kind heart does.

I'm not vain, at least I hope I'm not, but I so much wanted Luke to notice the new dress that Mama and I made. And, yes, for him to say I looked good in it. It's the shortest one I've ever worn, it's almost two inches above my knee, and I could tell Mama was not happy about that the first time I tried it on, but she didn't say anything—just gave me the "wrinkled brow" look. I know the dress is too short to wear to mass, and I've never worn a dress to school. I don't own any slacks; they're just too expensive and Mama says they're harder to make than a dress or skirt. Luke did compliment me on my dress and said I looked great in it and then started asking questions about how long it took to make and what it was made of—that type of thing. I felt like he was honoring me for the work Mama and I put into making it.

When we got to the restaurant and started looking over the menu, Luke confessed he needed help. He said he had been doing a lot of googling about restaurant food, but he was still confused. He confided to me that he had never eaten at what he called a "sit down, nighttime restaurant," that his mom and dad had always said those types of places were for folks "who put on airs." He also said he had never had a salad before, that he knew what one was, but didn't know what fork to use to eat one or what kind of "topping" to put on one. I could tell that he was embarrassed about his lack of knowledge about that type of thing.

He had told me before that the usual meal at his parent's house had been hot dogs, hamburgers, or pizza, or some cheap cut of fried meat and that a lot of dinners had just been macaroni and cheese or something frozen put in a microwave. That dinner had always been a stressful thing at his house and one time his dad had yelled at him for cutting the fat off a piece of meat and saying that he was not to "act all high and mighty in my house." Luke said a couple times they all went out to fast food joints, but that was only because they were going to or coming back from a car race when he was young. What they ate then was pizza or fried burgers or hotdogs just like at home. Luke rarely talks about his parents anymore, especially his dad. I know he misses his mom, but I'm really sure he doesn't miss his dad.

So I explained to Luke about what the different kinds of seafood tasted like and before I even got to the various cuts of beef, he decided that he wanted to try the seafood. He said he had had tuna before, but not very often, but I bet it was out of a can or pouch. He picked flounder almondine, and he said he would have it grilled. I had told him that it was healthier that way instead of being fried, and he grinned at me and said he already knew that. I think he also picked flounder because it was the cheapest seafood on the menu, and he didn't want to run up our bill. I picked the flounder, too. I also told him to choose French dressing for his salad. I just couldn't see him as an oil and vinegar guy.

The waitress came back, and we ordered and everything just went perfectly. Luke said he really liked salad and could I make ones for us the next time we went on a picnic. I said,

"How about next Saturday?" and he started teasing me about being too "forward" because he knows I worry about that all the time. But, actually, since we've been going together, sometimes I plan things and sometimes he does and sometimes we both do. I think that's the way it should be between two people dating, that both members of the couple should feel free to make suggestions.

The flounder was great, too, and so was the baked potato and steamed vegetable medley. When we were done with the main course, the waitress came by and dropped off the dessert menu. We had never discussed having dessert and how much that would cost and we knew that we had to give the waitress a tip and things just started seeming more and more expensive, so we both decided to tell the waitress we were too full to eat dessert.

After we left, it was still early, and I didn't want to go back to Camila's house so soon. I wanted to spend time with him. And Luke did the nicest thing. He stopped at the Dairy Queen, and said we were going to eat ice cream there as our dessert and he was treating and that was the end of the discussion. It was so like him. I had a chocolate ice cream cone and Luke, as always, had a vanilla one.

I don't care that Luke doesn't know how to dress up or how to order at a restaurant. I can teach him those things. His heart is in the right place, that's for sure, and that's all I care about. After he escorted me to the door, we kissed each other for the longest time.

Who Am I?

Chapter Fifty-Three: Luke

I had almost forgotten about Thomas' threat to beat me up, but he was kind enough to remind me of that fact last Tuesday during lunch went I went to the restroom before heading to the library. I am washing my hands when the next thing I know someone slugs me in the back from behind, puts an arm lock on me and snaps out, "How ya been," and twirls me around, and I see he's brought along two of his buddies.

I'm plenty scared, I'll admit that. My back is just killing me and Thomas is a good 40 pounds heavier and three inches taller than me. He could play football if he wasn't so stupid in all his classes... he's got a tight end-type build. "Ready to do this thing, boy?" he asks.

All kinds of things start rushing through my head. I can't take him on one-on-one, and I sure as heck can't beat him and his two fellow jerks. Then I realize how this whole thing is probably going to go down. His two buddies are going to hold me down or against the wall or stalls or something and Thomas is going to pound me to a pulp. I then see that one of his buds, Coby, has whipped out his phone and is filming the whole thing... which is just freaking unbelievable. I'm going to star in an Instagram video. Is Thomas too stupid to realize that some school administrator could see that? Apparently so.

"Answer me, Luke," he asks again and jerks my arm hard, and now my back and left arm are both shooting pains all over my body. "Are you ready to get down, boy?"

I've got to think fast, I know that. If I say something sarcastic, I could really set Thomas off. My next thought is to say something like, "So it's going to take three of you to beat somebody up that's smaller than all of you." But that's sarcastic, too, and Thomas isn't interested in a fair fight. He's not lying, all he really wants to do is beat the crap out of me. Finally, I say, "If we fight, we're both going to get suspended." Yep, that's what would happen. I would get suspended for being beaten up because there's no witnesses to say otherwise because for sure my three "friends" here are going to claim that I started the whole thing.

All of a sudden, Thomas shoves me toward his other JD, Lance, who holds me while Thomas pounds me three times in the stomach. I can't breathe, I'm in such agony. I'm all doubled over, and I hear Coby shout out, "Great stuff, keep hitting him." Yep, I'll be an Instagram sensation in about five minutes.

Then Thomas puts his face right tight to mine and says, "I've been easy on you, boy. Tell you what I'm going to do next. I'm going to count to 10 and then I'm going to start hitting you in the face for a while. Lance, how many times should I hit him in the face? Five, 10, 15?"

"Let's go for 10," says Coby and then Lance says something under his breath, I don't remember what.

Next, Thomas takes a hold of my hair and wrenches my head upward and again puts his foul mouth up next to me. "Is 10 about right, how many teeth can I knock out if I hit ya 10 times?"

I'm shaking like crazy now. I can't help it, I'm super scared and then I luck out. I mean I couldn't belief it, but thinking about it now makes sense. It's lunchtime, guys are going to be going to the restroom. Thomas was smart enough to figure out that I always go to the bathroom before heading to the library but he was too stupid to realize that other guys go then, too. Joshua, Marcus' brother, comes through the door, sees what's going on, and rushes over to where they're holding me. Joshua's a big dude; heck, he's a man. The next thing I know, they've let go of me, I've slumped to the floor, Joshua is yelling curses at Thomas and his friends, and they're running out of the restroom. My ribs are absolutely killing me.

Joshua helps me stand up and supports me until we get to the nurse's office where he leaves me and says he's going to report the whole thing to Mr. Caldwell. I tell the nurse about my ribs, and she feels around for a while and says it looks like they're just bruised. She calls Granddaddy and he comes to pick me up, and we go to the doctor. Yep, it was bruised ribs. I'm lucky it was nothing worse and that Joshua came in and saw what was happening before my face was rearranged. That's twice this year that Joshua has saved my butt.

Thomas got 10 days of suspension, Coby and Lance five each. They both ratted on "their best friend," saying it was his fault that the whole thing happened, that they never actually hit me. What a surprise that they would try to save their own skins. I spend two days on the couch and have to postpone mowing two lawns. I don't regret taking up for Ms. Waters that day in the classroom, which is what started this whole mess. I know who I am. Yeah, I would have hit Thomas if I'd had to. But I'm not a fighter. The last time I got into a fight was when I was 10. Allen and I were playing checkers in his backyard and this stupid nine-year-old kid Steven, who was watching, started knocking them off the board. He did that two times, and I told him the next time he did that, I was going to beat him up. And Steven knocked them off a third time, and I beat him up until he went home crying.

But fighting is kid stuff and it never really settles anything. I want more things out of life than settling scores with punks like Thomas. I really do think I know who I am now.

Chapter Fifty-Four: Elly

Can you believe it! I'm Caleb's girlfriend, that's who I am! I've wanted this for so long, but I never believed it would happen. I mean, he is absolutely the best looking guy in the sophomore class, he's the quarterback for the football team, all kinds of girls want to date him. He even goes to my church and my parents are friends with his parents. I mean it's absolutely perfect.

It all happened so suddenly. The day after prom, Mary, who always knows about this kind of stuff before anyone else, texted me and said that Caleb had broken up with his junior girlfriend and he had asked her about how serious I was about Eric. And she said that I wasn't interested in Eric anymore, which is obviously true, and she knew for a fact that I thought Caleb was a "very special guy." That was just the perfect thing for Mary to say—not make it so obvious that I have had a long time thing for Caleb.

A couple of hours later I got a text from Caleb and we started texting back and forth for several hours on Saturday and then that evening, I got a text from him, asking "R u going to church on Sunday, do u wanna sit together?" Honestly, I had planned to sleep in that morning, but I texted back "Yes and yes." Sitting next to him was so exciting. He dresses so sharp, that curly blonde hair, those muscles, I mean every high school girl in church that day must have been jealous of me. After church, he asked me if I wanted to go get something to eat, and I said I would have to ask my mom. So I walked over to her while she was going to the car and asked her about it, and she gave me this huge smile and said, "That would be wonderful, good for you."

I thought we were just going out for coffee or something like that, but instead we went out to a really nice restaurant. Caleb explained that since we were all dressed up for church, why not go out somewhere nice for our first date. I was so thrilled when he called it a date. I mean if we had gone out for coffee, that would have made it seem more like we were just in the talking stage. After we ate, we went driving out in the country and after a while, Caleb pulled over at one of those scenic overlooks and said let's take a look at the scenery. But we had only been there for a little while that he started kissing me and telling me how beautiful I look and what a great figure I have. I do, too. I'm not a wallflower anymore with mousy glasses and chubby legs.

When Caleb dropped me off at my house, he asked if I was free on Friday night to go out again, and I said yes. I didn't care where we were going. We ended up going out to eat again, and then we drove to that same overlook again and made out. When he was kissing me, it was the most wonderful thing. Saturday we went out to a movie and on the way there, he told me that he wanted us to be official... to not date anyone else, "Would you be down with that?" he asked.

I said that would be wonderful and now we've had five dates and things have just been great. Caleb mostly talks about how great things are going to be for him and the football team this fall. How he wants to play college and pro football and how much money he can make in the pros. You know, when I was dating those other athletes and they would ramble on and on about sports, I just couldn't stand it, it was so boring. But somehow listening to Caleb is so different. I mean I have to pinch myself sometimes to think that we're together, and, again, it was so sudden. He's been telling me how much he wants to see me in a bikini this summer, and we ought to go to his parents' country club this summer and swim and sunbathe and take a rowboat around the lake. It is so romantic to think about spending the day with him and that night go paddling around a lake with the moon above, and, like, WOW!

The only down thing about Caleb and me being a couple is how Paige and Mia have been acting about the whole thing. Mia hasn't said much at all about it, but she always frowns when I start raving about how perfect Caleb is. I try to get her to say something about him, and she just acts evasive and won't say anything good or bad about him and our being a couple.

Paige, though, has been a little hurtful. One time when the three of us were talking, and I brought up Caleb, Paige said, "Are you really sure that dating him is a good thing, a smart thing to do. You know, he has a reputation for cheating on his girlfriends."

I know all that, she doesn't have to say stuff like that. But Caleb would never cheat on me. I told her that, too and she said, "Elly, you're not thinking straight. You're blinded by his good looks and the idea of dating him."

I got furious when she said that and then I asked Mia how she felt, and she wouldn't comment at all, but I got the impression that deep down she agreed with Paige. I don't care what they think. I'm Caleb's girlfriend, that's who I am.

Chapter Fifty-Five: Marcus

My head and body are so mixed up these days that sometimes I don't seem to know who I am anymore. The other day I was able to go to school for every period, but when I got home I went to my room and fell asleep and didn't wake up until around 8. I went downstairs to find something to eat and I heard Mom say my name to Dad, so I started listening to what they were saying.

My parents were having a discussion about whether or not I should play football this fall, assuming my leg is healed all right. But Mom was against my playing no matter what, saying it was too big a risk while Dad was countering that no decision had to be made right now. Mom wasn't having any of that, though, and kept hammering away to Dad that I could have permanent damage if I got another concussion.

How about my opinion on playing football, don't I get a say in this at all? It's my sports future that we're talking about here. Then I heard Mom say that Coach Dell was very worried about the "lingering effects" from the concussion, and he had told her the final decision on whether or not I played this coming year should be made by my parents, not by him or the coaching staff. Has everybody lost their freaking minds over my concussion?

Still, a few days later I got to thinking that maybe I should talk to somebody about how I should be preparing for college if I can't play pro ball. I mean, I've never worried about that before. My attitude last year was that high school classes didn't really matter since I was going to make a living playing sports. That doesn't seem like such a good plan now. My favorite teacher this year has been Mr. Wayne in World History, Part II, so I went to him Tuesday before class and asked if I could come in on Wednesday morning before school and talk about getting ready for college. He said that he would be glad to help me.

On Wednesday, I told him that there was a chance that I might be through with sports and did he think I could major in history in college.

"Don't give up on athletics so quickly," said Mr. Wayne. "You're only in tenth grade and people do get injured and come back from that, you know. You're a high caliber athlete, don't throw in the towel. Don't get discouraged."

When Mr. Wayne said all that, I got really encouraged about my sports future. But then what he said next, really discouraged me. I'm sure he didn't mean for what he said to be that way, but it felt like a kick in the gut.

"I've taught some very good athletes," he said. "One of them tore up his knee really bad like you did and had to be a freshman walk-on for his college football team and actually made the team. By the time he was a senior, he had a scholarship."

So, now, I can set my sights on being a walk-on, and if I try really, really hard, by my senior year in college, maybe I can be a backup player who is given a pity scholarship? Is that what I have to look forward to?

"It's good that you're thinking about your college classes more, no matter what happens with sports," he continued. "I think you'd really enjoy being a history major. You're one of my best students. When you're applying to colleges, come to me and I'll write a great reference for you."

When Mr. Wayne said all that, it made me feel better. Next, I asked him what kind of jobs I could do besides teaching which I obviously knew was available. He said I could work at a museum, be a librarian or a curator. I could be a researcher or a para-legal or even get a law degree after I majored in history which is what some lawyers do. So what should I do to be getting ready to maybe be a history major?

"Start reading more outside of class on your own," Mr. Wayne said. "When I told one of my teachers about my wanting to major in history, she suggested I read *For Whom the Bell Tolls* by Hemingway. The book is about the Spanish Civil War, but it is also about the horrors of war in general. I learned a lot from that book. I bet you would, too. When you read it at night, come on in the next morning before school and we can talk about what's going on."

Mr. Wayne then said if I wanted to read another good book about war to try *A Bright Shining Lie* about the Vietnam War, which we had just finished studying. I think that book might be interesting, too. When I was running all that through my mind, Mr. Wayne started talking again.

"Look, Marcus, I know you're really worried about your concussion, and, yeah, life sometimes sucks," he said. "But I really think, in the end, things will turn out fine for you, regardless of whether you play sports or not. You've got a good head on your shoulders. You've got great parents and a great brother. I taught Joshua, too, and I know he's someone that you can go to for advice. Come to me anytime. I'll be glad to listen and help if I can."

That morning, Mr. Wayne threw a lot out to me. I've got a lot of thinking to do about my future. I'm going to check out those two books from the library, first chance I get. I may not know who I am yet or what I'll do if sports don't work out, but at least I've got some options now.

Chapter Fifty-Six: Mia

Lately, I've been doing a lot of thinking about my future. Ms. Whitney says that junior year is the most important one in high school. That's the year when we should start seriously thinking about our futures and about what we're going to do after high school, whether it's going to college or trade school or the military or the workforce. I've known since forever that I was going to college, but I've decided for sure now that I want to be a pediatrician.

I've just got to do something that will make a difference in people's lives, especially kids. Mama and Poppa have told me so much about how hard life is for our family members in Texas and Mexico that I'd like to go live in one of those places and work with underprivileged, rural kids who need quality health care worse than just about anyone. I've read that the poor, rural parts of the country don't have many doctors, and the ones that are around are stretched really thin.

I told Ms. Whitney about my plans, and she suggested that I should participate in the school's STEM program my junior and senior years and take those science, technology, engineering, and math classes to help me prepare for a career in medicine. That means, I would be off the school campus for half a day, but I could still take English, history, and Yearbook in the afternoon. I would at least have Yearbook class with Luke seventh period, and that would be great.

I told Luke that now I've definitely decided to be a doctor and about taking STEM classes and living somewhere else besides here when I finish all those years of schooling. He was very enthusiastic about my plans and told me to "Go for it!" I was really glad when he said all that. But I wanted him to add something like, "I bet it would be nice to live in the Southwest," or something like that, but he didn't say anything about living so far away.

Luke and I've talked many times about our being too young to know what love is, and I know we are really too young to know. But we're being told that we have to start making all these adult-type decisions now to prepare for college and our futures, yet we're also being told that kids our age don't know what true love is. Why are we supposed to know about our futures when we're still in tenth grade, but we're not capable of knowing what true love is? I know the two things aren't the same, but I do know that Luke shows me he has all the things that I would want from a husband: respect, kindness, empathy, affection... he listens to me and wants to know what I think about things.

Maybe, I shouldn't be thinking too much about a possible future with Luke, maybe I should just let things develop and see what happens between us. I can't ever see breaking up with him, though. But I can't see someone like him wanting to live in the Southwest and how hot and flat so much of that country is. He loves the mountains and roaming about in the winter; would he give all that up for me? Would it be fair of me to ask him if he would? I have told myself over and over to stop thinking about a possible future with Luke, but I keep speculating anyway. I should just let things evolve naturally. I know who I am and what my future will be, but I don't know if Luke will be part of that future. Will we still be together after high school... and after college?

After the school day where I talked to Ms. Whitney about STEM and becoming a pediatrician, I decided to announce my plans when Mama and Poppa and my sisters and I sat down for dinner that evening. When I told everyone, Mama said she was "absolutely thrilled" that I was going to become a pediatrician. She added, "Every day, you'll be making kids' lives better. I'm so proud of you!"

My sisters chimed in and said they were happy for me, too. Then I looked over at Poppa and asked him what he thought, and he just mumbled something and looked angry—maybe he had had a bad day at work. I looked over at Mama, and she asked if I still had the top average in my tenth grade class, was I still on track to be valedictorian? I told her that Ms. Whitney had brought the subject up, and that she had told me that I still had the best average.

I don't like to ask Ms. Whitney about my being the valedictorian; it sounds arrogant and conceited to be talking about it to other people. If it happens, it happens. I'm not going to base my life around being a valedictorian; having the top average in my class is not going to define me. But after my announcement, that's all Mama wanted to talk about. She said I maybe could get a full scholarship at some college because of my grades and teacher recommendations. That would mean that there would be more money for my sisters' educations. When she put it that way, I understood why she is so obsessed with my grades. But I still don't like to talk about being "the perfect student."

Poppa still hadn't said anything the whole meal, so finally I said, "Poppa, is something the matter? Are you okay?"

And he said that he had had an interesting discussion at work today with Camila's father. He said he had asked him if Camila's older brother—Miguel, he's a senior—was dating anyone and was told that he wasn't.

"I then told him that you weren't dating anyone and maybe our two children might like to go out together," said Poppa. "That's when he told me about how you and your 'boyfriend Luke' were kissing each other on his front stoop not long ago."

Last Week
of School

Chapter Fifty-Seven: Luke

The last week of school, especially the last two days, nothing much goes on, and a lot of kids skip. The state tests are all over and what happens if a kid is actually sick and misses the last couple of days. Are that kid and teacher going to meet up the next week and make up work? I don't think so. Everybody has either failed or passed by now, and there's nothing anyone can do about it one way or the other. I bet the teachers are probably as worn out as the students.

I've spent a lot of time recently talking to Granddaddy, Mia, and Mr. Miley, he's the cross country coach, about this summer and next fall. Granddaddy and Mia want me to give up the lawn business next fall and concentrate on my grades and running cross country. They both say that I made a good start this year on making better grades and if I played a sport, like cross country, I would stand a better chance of getting a scholarship to some college. It would show that I was more "well-rounded." I asked them both who was going to give me a scholarship with my low D averages every year in math?

I swear, they must have been talking behind my back because both of them gave the same answer… that my losing my parents and coming from a home without much money would help me to qualify for financial aid. Both of them said, and it's true, that my grades went up this year in spite of all that happened. I wouldn't mind if they had been talking behind my back. Both of them want what's best for me and I'm lucky to have Granddaddy and Mia around to help me. I know what would have happened to me without them. Living in a foster home, probably being bullied at a new school, and no Mia. I don't know if I could have survived all that.

I talked to Mr. Miley, and he said I had the speed and endurance to be a good cross country runner. The fact that I have been running for years on my own tells him plenty, he said, about what kind of effort I would make if I were on the team. I told him about what Granddaddy and Mia have been saying about my needing to participate in some extracurricular activities and he agreed with them. But before I committed to cross country, I had to talk one more time to Granddaddy about how we were going to afford for me to go to college, partial scholarship or not.

Granddaddy said we had that inheritance money in the bank from my parents dying—all that money is for me. It's not a lot, he said, but it would be enough to buy me a little land out in the country to live on one day. He knows how important that is to me. Granddaddy said then there's my lawn business money and the little that he has saved up and we could sell our house and live in an apartment if we had to. I know that he would make that sacrifice for me, that's one of many reasons why I love him so much. "One way or the other, we'll have enough for you to go to college," he said.

So I definitely have committed to running cross country in the fall. Mia and I will work extra hard this summer on our business because she's going to STEM this fall, and she doesn't think she will have time to do anything after school except study. Mr. Miley has given me a summer running regimen, which I can do in the mornings when it's still cool—that's my favorite time to run year round anyway. Granddaddy said we also could "seriously look" for a little parcel of country land for us to buy this summer. "Land's not going to get any cheaper, you know," he said, and he's right.

Mia told me that she has definitely decided to become a pediatrician and go live where her family members live in either Texas or Mexico. I said I was happy for her, and I am. She would be great at being a doctor for little kids. Later, I thought about living out there with her and whether I would be happy or not. Sometimes, I think what it would be like to be married to her. Yeah, guys do think about those sorts of things, especially after we've been with a girl for a long time. I mean we've dated since the school year started, but we've been a couple for way over a year. I can't imagine now what life would be like without having her to talk to every day and hang out together.

Neither one of us has ever said we love each other because we've agreed that we're too young to know and to not to use the word love "lightly" she says. She's right. But I have all these deep feelings for her, and sometimes I really, really believe that if that's not love, what is. We talk about what we're going to do our junior year together and maybe taking a day trip together one Saturday and sometimes we even talk about how we possibly could go to the same college. Some days, I see her as being *the one* forever. But other days I realize that neither one of us has ever dated anybody else. I mean as beautiful and as smart and kind as she is can you imagine how the guys in a college would be after her.

One night the last week of school I was lying in bed and thinking about all those things when Mia called me really late. She said her poppa had found out about us, and her parents were arguing really bad about us. She said her father was telling her mom and her that we had to break up, and her mother was saying that she really liked me and for her dad not to interfere and "let your daughter make her own decisions about boys." The fear of maybe losing Mia sent chills down my spine.

Chapter Fifty-Eight: Elly

Caleb got really angry at me on the next to last day of school. I was sitting with Paige and Allen in the cafeteria, and Paige left to go to the restroom, so it was just Allen and me. Since Caleb and I started dating, he expects me to eat with him at the "football players" table as everybody calls it. It's really awesome to sit where all the hot guys sit with their girlfriends. But earlier in the day, I had asked him if it would be all right if I came over later during lunch because Paige and I were going shopping after school for some summertime outfits, and we needed to plan out the stores we were going to hit and whether we should eat out or not. And Caleb had given me permission to do that for a while, then come sit with him and eat.

But when Caleb came over and saw me sitting with just Allen, he just went nuts. He snapped at Allen and said, "What are you doing sitting alone with my girlfriend!"

Alan tried to explain that the whole thing was innocent, that he was not horning in, that his girlfriend Paige had been there until just a second ago... those types of answers. Caleb was just furious, he was all red in the face. For a second, I was afraid that Caleb was going to hit Allen. About that time, Paige came back and that calmed Caleb down a little for a while. But then he got angry again and snapped at me to "Get up and come with me right now!" And I did.

I desperately don't want to lose him as a boyfriend after waiting so long for him to finally notice me and ask me out. I apologized and apologized to him on the way to the football table, telling him that the whole thing was innocent. He knows that Allen and Paige have been going together since near the start of freshman year. I would never cheat on Caleb. I've promised him that I wouldn't after he told me that he expected that out of all his girlfriends.

Normally, I go to a lot of enrichment-type camps and seminars and workshops every summer, but I've already cancelled going to one on photojournalism because he has a big party planned that same weekend at his parents' lake house. Ms. Hawk had told me about the photo thing and said that though I was a gifted photographer, this workshop would expose me to all kinds of new techniques. My cancelling that workshop alone should show Caleb how serious I am about our relationship. And his parents and my parents are going to share the same rental house at the beach for a week in July, which means we'll be spending every day together then… and every night. How romantic is that going to be! A week with Caleb at the beach: moonlight walks along the beach, swimming in the surf, going out to dinner at night, tanning by the ocean together… how great is that going to be! Wow, how many girls at school would like to trade places with me?

My parents are crazy wild about Caleb, saying how perfect he is for me, and his parents have told me that they are "thrilled" that we're going together, that it "should have happened long ago." Even my little brothers are happy about it. They keep asking me if Caleb can get them free football gear and tickets to NFL games when he is playing pro ball. I bet he can.

After we got to our table and Caleb had calmed down a little, I told him why I had been sitting with Paige and our going shopping after school. I also told him that I was going shopping for summertime outfits and had planned to take some of them to the beach to wear for him. He told me he can hardly wait to see me in a bikini and how great I look in short skirts and what super legs I have. I thanked him and thanked him for his compliments and promised him that I "wouldn't mess up again." He then gave me permission to go shopping with Paige because usually I ride home with him, since we live so close together. Riding the big yellow cheese is for kids anyway.

After school, I met up with Paige as we had planned and told her that Caleb and I had worked things out and I had apologized to him. "Apologized for what, him being a jerk?" she said.

I told her not to talk that way about Caleb, and Paige interrupted me when I was explaining, which was really rude of her. "Have you lost your mind, Elly," she said. "He's the one that ought to be apologizing to you and to Allen. No guy should treat a girl like that!"

Paige and Mia are my best friends, but I lost my temper when she said that about Caleb.

"Don't talk that way about him," I said, then I blurted out that Caleb has told me that he loves me.

"He says he loves you, after you two dating three weeks?" she said. "Get real, Elly, you have lost your mind. Do you even know the difference between lust and love?"

The next thing I knew we were arguing so bad that one or both of us said that we weren't going shopping together that afternoon and Paige turned away from me and stomped off. We've been best friends since fifth grade, and I don't want to lose that friendship, but she never should have criticized Caleb… that was way out of line.

That night I called Mia to ask her advice, but we hadn't even talked a minute when she started crying about her dad telling her that she has to break up with Luke but that her mom is saying that she definitely does not have to—her parents have been arguing all week about it. I'm glad I don't have that problem. My parents absolutely love my boyfriend.

Chapter Fifty-Nine: Marcus

The last day of school, I was sitting in Mrs. Roberts' geometry class and listening to music and basically just chilling when Caleb walked over to me and sat down. We've barely talked since football season ended. I think those bad feelings left over from that fight during football practice…well, I think they're still there. So I was glad when he walked over. When my concussion thing is over and my leg heals, Caleb and I are going to have to start communicating and talking about plays and stuff… assuming I'm going to play football this fall.

Caleb's first question was how I was feeling after all that I've gone through. Actually, the past few days have been the best I've felt since the injury. I've had only a few small headaches—and they didn't last long—and Mom and Dad say they can tell I'm "more on top of things." My leg feels much better, too. I'm walking around pretty normal. I'm not ready to do any running yet, but the school's trainer, Ms. Martin, has been checking with me every week; she's given me a series of exercises to strengthen my leg, and says I'm making very good progress. Every week she gives me stuff to do that's just a little bit harder than the week before.

I told Caleb all that, and he said "cool deal," and then he mentioned that there was a "real burner" coming up from middle school, his name is Tito, and that he and I could form one "dynamic duo" for him to throw to. I've heard about this Tito dude. Jonathan is going to have some serious competition at the other receiver slot, that's for sure. Caleb and I both agreed about that. "What I'd really like to do," said Caleb, " is run a three-receiver offense with you, Jonathan, and Tito. The other teams would never figure out who the hot receiver was."

We both agreed that that type of offense would be pretty much unstoppable, but Coach Dell has such a conservative playbook that he'd never go for it. Then Caleb said he had one more thing to discuss.

"You still have Tameka's number?" he asked. "When we double dated several times last year…, you know, she's pretty hot. You wouldn't mind me calling her, would ya?"

I said I hadn't talked to or seen Tameka since we broke up, her going to another school and all, but I still had her number, so I gave it to him. You know, I think the real reason he came over to me was not to check on my condition or talk about football, but to get that number. He's smooth alright. I was smooth, too, last year, but it didn't bring me anything except misery with girls. You know, I don't think Caleb has grown up one bit this year, he's still operating like he and I did when we were freshmen. No wonder Joshua kept calling me *insufferable* last year.

"Thanks, man," Caleb said when I gave him Tameka's number. "Maybe, she and I can double date with you and Kylee this summer."

"You're pretty confident she'll go out with you, aren't ya," I said.

"Get real, Marcus, of course, she'll go out with me, duh," he said.

Yep, that's how I would have acted last year if I had been in his shoes, all cocky that girls were just waiting around, hoping for me to text them. Doesn't he realize that Kylee and Elly are friends and that for sure Kylee would tell Elly about Caleb cheating on her? I mean, how dumb can he be. He knows how girls are about that type of thing.

So I told Caleb that Kylee and me wouldn't be interested in double dating with him and Tameka, that we just liked doing stuff by ourselves. That I had a lot of stuff to do this summer with rehabbing and all that.

"I feel you, I got you," he said with this smirk and then he walked away. What a jerk. He was just using me, like he uses girls and everybody else. I do have a lot of things to do this summer, besides rehabbing. After talking to Mr. Wayne a lot, I decided to take his elective class, Conflicts in American History. He said that would help me prepare for being a history major in college. I finished reading *For Whom the Bell Tolls* already. It was fantastic. Like the book says "No man is an island," and "Any man's death diminishes me." Most wars are stupid and pointless, especially for the soldiers out on the battlefield…they're just like chess pawns. And all those things that happened in the 30s and 40s are still important today, because the "arc of history," as Mr. Wayne says, is "still sorting things out." I never knew before that this history thing could be interesting, but it really is.

I've got to read two books for English AP next year: *I Know Why the Caged Bird Sings* (finally a book by a black author) and *Pride and Prejudice* (I've heard that it's pure "chick lit," but I guess I can stand it). I'm going to read every bit of these books, too. I've learned my lesson about screwing around in school.

This summer, I'm going to get my leg right, and my head right, and I'm going to get my reading done. And I'm going to spend as much time as I can with Kylee.

Chapter Sixty: Mia

I've never been so angry and upset in my whole life. Every day this week since Poppa found out about Luke and me, when Poppa and Mama have gotten home from work, he asks me if I've broken up with Luke yet. Then Mama interrupts him—which makes him mad—and says that "We have gone all over that, and I've told you that he's a nice boy." My parents spend much of dinner arguing and the house is just in an uproar. I hate seeing my parents fight over me and sometime every evening, I go to my room and cry.

It's so unfair. Poppa is treating me like a kid. I work all the time, and I don't think he appreciates it much. Every evening I either make dinner or help Mama cook when she gets home. I take care of the chickens, doing most all the work. I do a lot of the yard work. I babysit every Friday and Saturday night and sometimes on Sunday afternoons. I'm tired all the time from studying or working. Both my parents are constantly harping that I have to be valedictorian, and I keep telling them I can't be any higher in the class rank than I already am. All this week, I've felt constant pressure, especially from papa.

And all I am asking to do is spend a few hours on Saturdays being with Luke—that's all I'm asking, and my father won't even give me that much so I can have a little bit of a life. I've been the most "perfect American daughter" and it's still not good enough for him. He keeps asking if Luke has shown disrespect for me, and I keep telling him that he hasn't and then Poppa goes on and on about "how white boys like Luke are," and I just hate it—that stereotyping of people. I get it that Poppa has put up with a lot of prejudice at his various jobs. I get it that lots of people show him disrespect because he's a Mexican and he's done nothing but manual labor his whole time in America. But that's not Luke's fault. It's not Luke's fault that he had a bad home life growing up. I tell Poppa that Luke now has a very stable life living with his grandfather, and that his grandfather has been very kind to me and likes me. I keep telling him that Luke is going to college and works really hard at our business. But nothing I say seems to matter to him.

On Wednesday, I came up with the best idea I could think of to convince Poppa that Luke and I should stay together— that if we broke up we would have to dissolve our L&M business and that would really hurt my income since I would miss out on all the referrals that Luke sends me. But even that didn't faze my father. He kept saying I could make up the lost money in other ways and I kept replying "How am I supposed to do that, walking up and down the street knocking on rich people's doors and begging for them to let me babysit?"

He yelled at me and told me not to "get sarcastic" with him. I was so upset, Poppa had never yelled at me before this week and rarely had he and Mama ever argued about anything—now that's all they do. Friday night, after I came home from the last day of school, we had another argument filled dinner and it was the worst one yet. As usual after the usual accusations had been made, we finished eating in silence; after dinner, I went to my room to cry—as usual. I just can't help it. But this time, Mama came into my room about 15 minutes after I did.

I was stretched out on my bed, sobbing face down in the sheets when Mama started talking.

She said, "I can't go on like this. Your poppa and I argue on the way to work, on the way home from work and all during dinner and after. You know how much I like Luke, and I know

I trust you and him. But your poppa and I can't go on like this. He's not going to give in on this."

I thanked her and thanked her for taking my side, and I told her again how much Luke means to me and how good we are together. I explained to her—again—that I don't know if we have a future together after high school, but that we need to make that decision, not Poppa. And she said again that she and Poppa couldn't go on fighting like this and that he wasn't going to give up on ending Luke's and my relationship.

It was about an hour later when I had stopped crying and was thinking straight that I finally realized what she had meant. That she and I not giving in on the Luke thing could maybe cause Mama and Poppa's marriage to fall apart. Was she hinting that it would be my fault if that happened? Was she suggesting in a subtle way that the right thing for me to do was to break up with Luke, for the sake of our family? That I was being selfish if I kept seeing him? I don't know what I'm going to do.

ABOUT THE AUTHOR

Bruce Ingram is a high-school English teacher and lifelong outdoorsman who has written five well-reviewed river guides set in his native Virginia. *Tenth Grade Angst* is the sequel to his debut novel, *Ninth Grade Blues,* published in 2017.